AGENTS
OF
CHANGE

JACK KING

DEDICATION

This work of fiction is dedicated to all agents of change

"Be a patriot - kill a priest."

A slogan used by death squads.

1. Demon in the Skin of an Angel

He shuddered to think her name lest the incantation awaken the spirit of pain and misery. Only when the airliner took off and rose to the heavenly heights so did his heart. With the distance between the den of the Beast and the aircraft growing so did his courage, and he brought himself to look at her. She was a demon in the skin of an Angel. Her tropical lagoon eyes were closed, and he savored the moment to observe her unawares, his eyes glazing over the tan skin of her slender neck, and sliding down to the valley of pleasure heights. Nestled in the narrow seat, her head on a soft pillow, she appeared benign and innocent. The innocence vanished in an instant when their elbows brushed on the seat divider. She jerked her arm as though the mere touch of his skin caused the hot embers inside her to inflame. The skin behind her ears ignited, the effect intensified by the hair, which resembled a field of wheat at harvest time. Suddenly he felt utterly and completely under her spell.

She opened her eyes and caught his gaze.

He blushed, angry for allowing her to catch him at a moment of weakness.

"I look forward to working with you, Hollie—" he uttered.

The hot lagoon in her eyes froze, but her whisper was scalding, "My name is no longer Hollie."

It took years of training and the collective strength of his brothers to withstand the torrid remark and the icy glance. Did she see through him? Did he allow the woman to pierce his impenetrable façade, to gaze into his soul? He was a master of micro-expressions, applying faces at will, according to circumstances, able to remain bland in the most dire of circumstances, or put on an appearance of happiness, sadness, or distress when the situation called for the opposite. He had faced exposure before, even death, and both he took without so much as a blink. But this was different. Never before did he find himself attracted to, and magnetically drawn to his enemy. Seated next to him, shoulder to shoulder, was a woman whose proximity made his hair stand up high in areas of his body he never suspected of being hirsute. Here was the one person who could break his cover and obliterate years of painstaking clandestine work. Here was a woman with the face of an angel, a woman whose one word could unleash misery upon the countless wretched souls for whom he and his brothers were the only hope.

He sighed. He was attracted to her, and the newly born affection was beginning to weaken his defenses. He realized with resignation that only a complete separation of feelings from objectives guaranteed the success of his mission. A mission, which began with the mark of an upturned cross penciled on the menu of the Ground Zero Café…

2. The Dead Drop

Yesterday...

"Gen. Platt would be proud of you, Karin."

Col. Clarence Clooles slipped his left arm into the sleeve of the coat the woman held for him.

"I'm the son he never had."

Capt. Karin Platt forced a smile and helped him with the right arm, her eyes remaining sober and diverted.

"Ah, but you're the daughter he always wanted."

The colonel returned the smile and slipped on the left-hand glove, his right one remaining bare for the biometric scanner.

He added, "You're as devoted and hard working an officer as he was."

"Duty before pleasure, such are times we live in."

Capt. Platt passed on the hat to her superior officer.

"There must be something better for a young woman to do on a Friday night."

The colonel put on the hat and took the briefcase the woman readied for him.

He turned to face his assistant, and said with a troubled smile, "I promised Dorothy I would not make you stay this late, day after day—"

"I'm almost done," Karin's voice betrayed impatience.

"Promise?" his voice lacked the pressure his words suggested. He had grown to rely on his assistant, her devotion allowing him to delegate more tasks away from his desk. "Till Sunday then. Dorothy came up with a new twist to her salmon rolls…"

Karin forced another smile and saw the officer to the door. Theirs was a relation not unlike one between family, but the coming Sunday would be the first day in months for Karin to look the Clooleses in the eyes without the underlying shame. She did not expect what the fateful day, all those months ago, would do to her conscience. The time she accepted the first envelope of tightly packed banknotes was the first in a long string of months marked by emotional torment. She had to lie to the Clooleses who treated her as their own daughter since Gen. Platt's passing. She hated herself for deceiving the colonel who became a father to her, and a grandfather to her daughter. He was also responsible for shaping Karin's career. He brought her to the Building, and made her his assistant. Without his and Dorothy's gentle intervention Karin would not have beat the depression she suffered following her parents' tragic passing. Worse still — her illness could have taken the life of her unborn daughter had the Clooleses, a childless couple, not stepped in and nurtured her until she was able to repay the only way she knew how — by letting them treat her as daughter and treating them as family in return.

Karin shook her head to shrug off the painful memories. She could not afford to unglue, not now when she faced the last chance to repay her debts and reconcile with her betrayal. She had thirty seconds to act.

Thirty seconds was all it took the colonel to cross the hallway to the bulletproof, hermetically sealed exit, where biometric scanners verified his identity. It took thirty seconds, thirty-five at the outside, before one scan of Clooles's palm would automatically shut down his computer terminal, and the safe inside his desk.

In two quick steps Karin approached the large oak desk topped with a framed photograph of Mrs. Clooles. She avoided looking into the still face, as though it was a portal into the living. At times of extreme stress Karin became superstitious and did not want to tease her fate, she could not bear it if her activity became known to the only people she cared about.

With a firm jerk she opened the right-hand cabinet door exposing the concealed safe with an electronic keyboard. She keyed in the sequence — a rotating set of birthdays of Karin and her daughter — taking longer than it took her on a regular day, such was her concern not to make a mistake she would not have time to correct.

The door popped open. Inside were a stack of folders, a book containing the colonel's encryption codes, and a tiny digital flash drive with a built-in palm scanner. Karin picked up the latter, grasping it tightly in the palm of her hand, and slammed the safe closed. She remained motionless for a time, pressing the clenched fist into her gasping chest. Seconds later she heard the characteristic click, followed by a hum of electronic equipment powering off — the sign that the safe and the computer terminal shut down until Monday, whereby the procedure would be reversed and she would replace the drive before the colonel walked into the office.

She remained on the floor until she regained control of her breath. She opened her fingers and looked at the object in her hand. This was her ticket out. By stealing the digital drive Karin promised herself to end the treacherous game. She understood the importance of the information contained inside it from the excitement she detected in her contact. She would demand an appropriate award. This time it would not be cash. She already paid off her debts. This time she would demand a way out.

She slipped the flash drive into a small self-sealing bag coated with a chemical compound, which made the contents undetectable to security scanners, and slipped it into her coat pocket. She checked out for the day, and trotted the corridor to the A Ring, forcing herself to walk slowly in order not to raise attention to herself. She took the staircase to a landing between the floors where, underneath the window facing the courtyard, stood a large marble pot with tropical plants in bloom. Karin stopped briefly to smell the flowers, as she did almost daily, consciously making it part of her routine. As she leaned against the container her right hand felt along the edge and the small self-sealing bag slipped unobtrusively into a dark crevice between the marble planter and the plastic lining of the drainage tank.

Pvt. Kamil Dorn stayed late in the office that night. His duties were not bound by the 9-to-5 constraints of the civilian workplace, yet he had not worked for the past two hours. Instead he spent the time pacing nervously to and fro. He had been waiting for the drop since lunchtime when the agreed upon signal — an upturned cross — appeared on the main menu of the Ground Zero Café. Today was the day the asset would make the delivery. It was not a routine drop as were so many before it. Dorn had picked up countless deliveries overtime, always on his way out of the office, at the end of his long shift. But not this time. Something unusual had happened. It was already three hours past the time the drop was supposed to have been made yet the item was not there. His anxiety was not helped by the authorization to use all means, even at the risk of exposing himself, to extract it. He had checked the agreed-upon dead drop location twice already, and was wary of drawing attention to himself — a uniformed soldier returning to smell flowers was not a sight the security was used to. Telling himself not to panic did not help. It was true that spying in the heart of the Superpower was not an easy task and one had to scout just the right moment to pass the secrets. Too he knew the asset worked for a workaholic for whom nine-to-five was a concept too liberal to apply to the military in general and to the military intelligence in particular. But rationalizing in the face of a breakthrough drop did little to calm his nerves. He had to summon the mantra imprinted in his memory at the intelligence school and supported by experience: Spying was more often a waiting game than an opportunity to display one's physical aptitude.

He left his office for the third and last time at 2200 sharp, and with an overwhelming conviction of something having gone wrong. Nonetheless he was determined to check the dead drop one last time. He had to. Too much depended on the success of the operation to give up in the face of a first hiccup. It took him four minutes to reach the correct staircase and several seconds to casually descend to the landing. He placed his attaché case on the edge of the marble planter as though looking for the gloves before stepping out into the frigid February night. His anxiety vanished instantly when his fingers clad in thin leather gloves felt the small object in the crevice.

Dorn glided down the last flight of stairs into the mezzanine, gleaming with relief, the small self-sealing bag inside his glove. He pulled his hat tight and joined the stream of personnel who were heading out into the blowing snow when his peripheral vision registered abnormality in the surroundings. Slightly to his right, ahead of him, three armed Naval security officers had approached a female officer whose back was turned to Dorn. Something clasped his throat when another officer stepped out from behind the security detail, his appearance causing the woman to freeze. Her consternation lasted a moment and was replaced by a reflex gesture, not unlike that of a stray dog before a flayer's halter tightens around its neck. Dorn gasped as the woman turned her head when he passed her. He thought she was looking into his eyes, but it was not so. Her gaze was penetrating through him, into the night outside. The woman was gazing into the outside world, her eyes desperate and longing, the eyes of someone who would not see the outside world for a long time. In those eyes Dorn recognized Karin Platt.

3. Ad Maiorem Dei Gloriam

The elderly man broke one of the cardinal rules of clandestine activity by remaining at the prearranged location long past the scheduled exchange. He should have left the scene when his agent failed to arrive within a specified timeframe. Spying in the capital city was a risky affair, and many agents who disregarded basic precautions had paid for it. Caution was key to a long spying career. The elderly man was an experienced agent. He had survived in the field for decades, in part because he observed the basics of the spying craft. This time, however, he disregarded precaution. The stakes justified the highest risk.

For this he would pay the highest price.

It happened without warning and it was over in seconds. He felt their presence, but he did not see the assailants charge. It felt as though a damp cold veil suddenly covered his shoulders. He turned his head and saw the light, not unlike the one, which is said to guide one to the great beyond. The light grew and split two ways, joined by a beastly roar of a heavy engine. Several men emerged and rushed toward him. He recognized their guttural accent and sudden peace filled his heart when he realized the end has come. He did not cry and did not plea when they picked him up and shoved inside. Resistance would not do, for no one who fell into their claws was ever seen alive again. He was not afraid to die. Life-long service taught him that death from their hands was merciful, but he knew they would have no mercy for him. He knew he would die in pain, and while he reconciled with a martyr's death as his destiny, as did so many of his predecessors, the Company explicitly forbade such sacrifice. Not because the Company did not trust its members to endure such test, but because torture would count against the perpetrators come Judgment Day when, God knows, they would have enough to answer for, anyway.

He clenched his teeth as soon as they picked him up and threw him into the vehicle. He felt the uncomfortable crunch when the faux tooth broke. He paused for a moment so as not to draw their attention. Then slowly, with the tip of his tongue, he felt for the tiny capsule in the cavity, taking every precaution not to choke on the broken tooth matter.

Whether they saw his maneuvering, or expected something of the kind, it was too late to stop him. Their hands reached for his throat to prevent him from swallowing, but they were too late.

His teeth crushed the capsule before their arms reached his throat.

With a smile on his face, he murmured, "*Ad maiorem Dei gloriam…*"

* * *

The silver-haired man who witnessed the event did not doubt the fate of his abducted friend. Placed in his shoes he too would take the only exit, which guaranteed security for the Company and its members. As his friend who was, doubtless, with the Creator by now, he was not afraid of death by torture. After all this was how many of their predecessors perished in the line of duty and call, but the

10

times had changed since. Today's enemies knew ways of extracting information from the bravest of men, and the Company preferred its members did not undergo these modern techniques. He did not fear physical pain. Pain suffered by those whom he served made him stronger, their collective suffering empowered him. He was spiritually prepared to parry any such advances, which enemies could direct against him. He was confident that no enemy who was equipped with the wit and skill to match his could ever hope to outmaneuver him, to force him to give out the secrets of his mind. They knew it too, and they took to ways, which no human being, however physically fit, or spiritually motivated, could successfully withstand. At their disposal was an arsenal of pharmacological aids, which facilitated altering the mind of the victim, and allowed the perpetrators to probe the knowledge contained within. To prevent such intrusion every brother who was at risk of falling into the claws of the Beast carried a defense shield — a faux tooth with a tiny glass capsule. Alas it was also the defense of last resort and explained why the silver-haired man's cheeks streamed with tears. He knew his friend of fifty years took his life in order for the cause to live on, *ad maiorem Dei gloriam*.

4. Ichneumon

Kamil Dorn was careful in his clandestine activities. Taking to heart the basic rules of survival, he brought home none of that which could betray him. This included legitimate work, lest they use it against him. The decision made his home a place of refuge from the stress and the unknown — something so many double-agents and moles found themselves in to their greater chagrin. His home was the one place, which could not betray him. That cold February night, however, he was filled with doubt. Faced with a close encounter that was the arrest of his asset, Dorn lost self-confidence. He could not go home. He should not. He considered fleeing abroad, but several minutes spent outside, in the blistering wind, cooled his mind sufficiently to allow rational thought: Karin Platt did not know his identity. She was not arrested red-handed, while making the drop, else Dorn would have been detained too. Thus, he reasoned, there existed a chance he might yet survive unscathed. The risk was minimal, and worth taking in light of the condition of those whom he vowed to serve.

Conscious of the necessity not to stray from his routine, and especially on the day such as this, lest it alert the security, Dorn did what he did every night. He rushed into the subway, and headed home. Music poured out of his earbuds, though what played he could not tell for his mind was elsewhere. He stepped out of the subway and waited for his eyes to adjust to the darkness. No one followed him, no one stabbed him in the back, yet he felt none the safer. He scouted the surroundings of his apartment building for a quarter of an hour, before he deemed it safe and decided to proceed. The doors showed no signs of entry, and the tiny hair left in the frame was the confirmation.

The power of self-doubt was such that he set out to do what his subconscious told him was not necessary. He gathered a waste basket-full of various papers. Two minutes later, as he stood over the kitchen sink, lighting the papers aflame, Dorn was startled beyond his wits.

A man appeared at the entrance to the kitchen.

"Hello, Kamil."

Speaking with a mild and hard to place accent indicative of people who conversed in multiple languages, or who spent prolonged time without contact with their native tongue, the man approached with outstretched arms.

Long ago Dorn learned to expect the unexpected from this neatly dressed man of indeterminate age. That of all people this silver-haired guardian angel should appear at such a dramatic moment bordered on miraculous, but was not surprising.

"You should not have come, Brother Anselm. It is dangerous!" Dorn's tongue said one, but his mind thought something else: Oh, yes, you should have!

Dorn was overwhelmed by the unexpected presence of his old friend and mentor. He turned to the sink and flushed the ashes down, but more importantly he took the time to conceal his trembling hands. He realized the arrival of

13

Brother Anselm was not coincidental, and whatever had occurred this night would lead to more extraordinary events.

"I was worried. You did not show up at the exchange," said the elderly visitor.

Dorn leaned against the sink, suddenly stricken by the weight of events, which befell on his shoulders.

With his forehead pressed against the overhead cabinet, he replied, "I'm so glad you're here."

"What happened?" the man asked as gently as only he could.

"What happened?" Dorn repeated quietly. "I wish I knew the answer."

He pushed away from the sink and reached to a desk drawer, which was set aside on the counter. He emptied the contents — more paper matter — into the sink. He struck a match and set the lot on fire.

The man called Brother Anselm watched the flames grow large, casting colorful flicks on the walls of the small kitchen. Reflections danced on the glass panels of the cabinets and on the encrusted silver cross which hung around Dorn's neck, and was visible between the lapels of the unbuttoned uniform. The cross! He remembered the day he presented it to his young protégé. It was the day he encouraged the boy to drop out from the seminary and put his strengths to better use. That day Dorn became Ichneumon, that mythical creature who hunted snakes and vermin. The day Dorn departed the seminary he carried with him the cross — the only reminder of his true calling.

With the small fire subsided, and the papers turned to ashes, Dorn took a deep breath. Cautious as he was, never bringing home work-related material, he could not rule out the possibility of a determined investigator setting his sights on something else entirely, and use it against him. He burned receipts from coffee shops and grocery stores, taxis and the drycleaner; he even torched a coaster from a pub he visited occasionally, all of which his enemies would study in detail, in order to dissect his life, something he deeply feared, however well prepared was his identity.

Dorn turned the tap, and watched the second heap of ash disappear into the drain.

At last he turned to Brother Anselm.

"They've apprehended our asset inside the Building."

The elderly man remained as stoic as ever. In his pacifying tone he asked, "Is the Company jeopardized?"

Dorn thought a moment before replying.

"I don't know how much she knows, but she had access to very sensitive material." After a minute of thoughtful silence he added, "Perhaps we out to send a coded warning, via the radio, before they jam the signal?"

Brother Anselm projected a reassuring smile.

"My dear friend, I've been on this Earth long enough to learn a thing or two, and I can say with confidence that no power in the world would dare interfere with the radio."

Dorn dove into his mentor's eyes. He found in them the assurance needed to calm his senses. Of course he knew it too. No one would dare interfere with the official broadcast of the spiritual leader of more than a billion worldwide. The Radio was the official voice of the State, which traversed traditional boundaries. It's journalists reported from over sixty countries, in fifty languages, and tasked with its operation was the Company. Dorn recalled Father Leon of the seminary boasting about the Radio as the modern-day equivalent to the missionaries of centuries past. It carried the Word around the Globe. Father Leon did not tell the seminarians then, and Dorn learned later that the Radio was also the ideal medium for communicating messages to undercover agents, some of whom may have become exposed as a result of Karin Platt's fall…

Brother Anselm understood what troubled his young protégé. In short words filled with pain he described the abduction he witnessed not two hours earlier.

They did not mourn. Sacrificing one's own to save the lives of many was part of the service they each were devoted to.

"I hope his sacrifice was worth it." Dorn could not hide the bitterness; for his young age he had witnessed too many such sacrifices already.

He reached into his pocket and placed the small self-sealing bag on the counter.

"Is this it?" The miniscule size of the item, which had cost the life of his friend, took Brother Anselm by surprise.

"Karin Platt delivered plenty of top intelligence, but if one was to judge by the recent spike in communication, today's cache is of the most significance."

They each gazed at the object, and each understood what occupied the mind of the other.

"With the loss of the Brother—" the elderly man started.

"I'll do it!" Dorn jumped in.

"You don't know how dangerous it is," Brother Anselm protested with a particular spark in his eye.

"It must be done!" Dorn replied with determination. "Besides, just knowing you are involved makes any undertaking much more likely to succeed."

"Yes, yes, it must be done."

Dorn took a deep breath. Something in his visitor's voice made him pause and reflect. Suddenly, he understood.

Brother Anselm read his mind.

"A courier has been dispatched from Rome. The exchange was scheduled... there."

Dorn did not need to ask what the *there* meant. The expression in his friend's eyes and the tone of voice were telling enough.

"I'll do it, all the same!" Dorn reiterated in a voice of steel, but his reply was drowned in the sudden vigorous knock on the front door.

They stood motionless, startled. They listened intently, their eyes darting from one another and into the short hallway, which led to the door.

The knock was repeated. Then again. And again.

"Dorn! Open up!" a voice penetrated the walls.

Dorn recognized it. His heart froze.

"Quick!"

He led his companion to the bedroom, and the small window. He gazed outside before pulling the panel open. Outside, the dark steel fire escape was eerily quiet. With his service pistol in his outstretched arm he waited for a sign of trouble. Nothing happened. Why were they not shooting? Why were they not shouting?

"Clear," he whispered and extended a hand to help his elderly companion over the window sill.

He then wanted to follow.

He was met with resistance.

"No," Brother Anselm said. "I'll draw them out. You hide it!"

Dorn cursed.

The bag! He had forgotten it. He turned back, while Brother Anselm began to descend the steel staircase into the back alley. Dorn looked down. Before his friend disappeared into the darkness, Dorn heard his words.

"Hide it, or destroy it, before they use it to destroy us..."

"Dorn, open up! I can smell smoke! I'll break the door!"

The voice drew him back inside. He recognized it. He knew what the presence of its owner at his doorstep signified. For a brief moment he considered abandoning the package and following Brother Anselm. At that moment his eyes were fixed on the darkness outside, not unlike the eyes of Karin Platt. He heard a muted sound outside, something rattling, probably garbage tins, and he understood Brother Anselm was drawing attention to himself, buying him time. It tipped the scale and Dorn tiptoed quickly to the kitchen.

He grabbed the package, and stood undecided, his mind rushing. It did not take long to realize the futility of any attempt to hide it. The man outside knew Dorn had picked up a cache from the dead drop, and no place would withstand a thorough search, furniture by furniture, fixture by fixture, book by book, every molecule by molecule.

Dorn slipped the bag back into his pocket and glided to the bedroom where, in the bedside table, was a small device, no larger than a mobile phone. He kept it for an occasion, when the need should call for an emergency data obliteration. He often assumed he would use it to destroy his computer's hard disk drive, but since his employ in the Building, under the command of a demanding officer, he had not yet had time to use his computer for personal tasks. He removed the device from its dusty cover, slid the safety button to the armed position, and placed it in the pocket, next to the digital drive, his finger on the trigger. Should the worst come to worst, he reasoned, he would obliterate the data, come what may.

5. Trapped

Maj. Will Kachem was a mysterious persona, whose name terrified his enemies and colleagues alike. His successes — or rather the successes attributed to him, for true successes seldom become known in the world of intelligence — earned him well-deserved respect, but his personality, the way he carried himself and treated those who crossed his path, commanded nothing but fear. Maj. Kachem had the uncanny ability to make other feel uncomfortable, his shrewd eyes, and carefully articulated words wrapped in sentences that intimated suspicion, were a reason why most of the students and the cadre avoided close encounters with the officer. It was also the reason why most students at the military intelligence school, where Kachem taught, made every effort not to draw attention to themselves. All except Kamil Dorn.

Years ago, having learned the identity of his teacher, the Company instructed Dorn to orchestrate such conditions, which would prompt Maj. Kachem to single out his student.

Dorn succeeded admirably. He took active part in the classes by questioning and probing, standing out where others avoided the officer's eyes, and never opened their mouths unless spoken to. The impression made on the teacher was enough to earn Dorn an assignment to a unit, which proved a treasure trove of information valuable to the Company. The CounterIntelligence Field Agency, or CIFA, was not unlike the man who headed it — secret and secretive, despised and feared. Little was known about its role, and even those tidbits which had leaked out took the form of rumors. And the rumors were enough to earn a hefty share of criticism from civil organizations, which charged the agency with domestic spying, its tentacles present in every aspect of public and private life through the widespread encouragement of citizens to snitch on their neighbors. The scope of the program was hardly surprising to those who knew human nature, where one did not need pressure to become envious of one's neighbor, and so it was that CIFA's databases grew rapidly, encompassing data on an ever-growing number of individuals and organizations, earning the agency a nickname of the C-*KGB*-IFA, Now, its founder and Dorn's superior officer was hollering at his door.

"Cozying in for the night?" Maj. Kachem spat out as he pushed his way through the door, his eyes darting from one side to the other. He did not wait for an answer. "You can forget about it."

Dorn followed the officer into the living room, painfully aware of the intensity with which the Major scrutinized every corner of the small apartment.

"You live alone, Dorn?"

Kamil said nothing. It was no use for Kachem knew darn well every detail of his staff's private lives.

"No one to say goodbye to?" Kachem continued in his trademark fashion.

On an ordinary day, having grown used to this trait, which made Maj. Kachem so unpopular, Dorn would have shrugged and let the remarks pass without effecting his frame of mind. But this was no ordinary day, and Dorn's nerves were stretched to their limits. He struggled to act naturally in the presence of this man who was antipathetic inside and out. Neither tall nor short, Kachem was a skinny man with thinning hair, greased and combed toward the back of the small head. He was usually seen holding a half of a thick and unlit cigar between his yellow teeth. Kachem did not smoke, the cigar coupled with the hair served to convey an image of toughness that was otherwise not there, for if anything Kachem was conniving and shrewd before he was strong.

The Major's squinted eyes darted from one side of the living room to another when he added in a short voice resembling a pat of a gun, "You'll need a toothbrush." His nostrils expanded and contracted as he smelled for traces of smoke created by the documents burned in the sink, his eyes suddenly fixed on Dorn's with an ominous grin.

It took years of practice and natural disposition not to yield to intimidation. Dorn dressed as calmly as he could, taking special care to conceal the trembling of his hands.

No teams of armed security personnel awaited outside. Strange tactic, Dorn thought. Kachem must feel supremely confident to have brought no backup, as though his mere presence was enough to render any resistance futile.

On the street a lone uniformed man pushed himself off the hood of the dark sedan and stamped the cigarette butt under his heel before opening the door for the two.

Dorn entered, followed by Kachem. He was calm now, almost relieved, as a long time fugitive would when caught at last, his uncertain existence drawing to an end. The game was over. He was caught, though not in the way he always imagined it would happen. No shots were fired, no shouts accompanied the event. It was almost as though it happened in some old romance, between gentlemen, only Kachem was the farthest being from an epitome of a knight.

Dorn was surprised at the turn his reaction has taken. The emotional strain endured during months of leading a double life, months of watching his every step and every word, in order to hide his true mission, could at last be put to rest. It was strangely soothing. The only thing that pained him was the realization he had failed, not personally, but those whom he vowed to serve.

"You've been with the CIFA, what, four months?" Kachem's question came as though from the clouds.

What's the point replying, Dorn thought, they bloody well know how long. Then, suddenly, he changed his mind. He knew it was a part of the game to ask a ton of questions, to slip in factual information mixed with erroneous, to confuse the subject, to induce internal struggle. For some the braking point came quickly, whereas others took longer, still some endured beyond normal person's threshold of resistance, but eventually they gave in too. Everybody did. Dorn knew it, and he decided to fight, to hold off as long as he could. He reasoned he could always die when no other route existed. The Company would recuperate from the loss of an agent of his experience and position, it survived larger cataclysms in its five-hundred year history. With the tip of his tongue he felt the faux tooth at the back of his mouth.

"Five months to the day on March first," Dorn replied, recalling basic tactic from his R2I training.

Resistance to Interrogation class pointed out the main objective to buy time, and was not unlike the amphibology practiced by the Company agents.

"Offer ambiguous and doubtful answers laid with facts, which are verifiable, though perhaps outdated; employ words with double meaning", the instructor would stress out. "Be in control of your mind and you may outlast your oppressors, no matter what their interrogation tools and techniques", he used to say. "Some detainees pray, others count, still others attempt to induce a deep state of mind, which is removed from the world of the present; some escape into childhood memories, some relive blissful moments of days disassociated with the path they chose later in life. It is an art onto itself. To avert the mind from the inevitable psychological torture, which accompanies coercive interrogation, takes a strong and well-disciplined individual…"

"Before?" Kachem pried, his voice a single shot at the heart.

"Overseas," Dorn replied in like manner, as though in a duel.

"You mean — Rome." Kachem grinned and added ominously, "Come now. The Holy See is the reason I'm taking you in."

6. Speak of the Devil

With only the driver in the front, and Maj. Kachem beside him, and no additional security teams following, Dorn was on the verge of jumping out from the moving vehicle into the darkness. He saw himself land on the side of the road, in a masterful somersault he knew he was capable of, and disappear into the dark streets. He would have done it, perhaps, were it not for the ride having ended sooner than expected. The car pulled into a dark parking lot of an abandoned or otherwise closed and decrepit fast-food joint just as Dorn was musing about ways to escape the predicament. He struggled out of the vehicle making every effort not to draw attention to the peculiar way he carried his hand. Not for long — he thought when he realized where he was brought. Is this how it ends? In a dark alley, in a heap of garbage and rubble? He was not surprised. He thought about his end, who would not in his line of business? Being stabbed in the back in some dark alley was a fitting end for a secret agent. This reminded him of the kind of dark alley

24

where he expected to end his life some day. But there awaited a surprise. A limousine was parked behind the building, in a location darker still. A door opened, its emergency light illuminating the pavement in a bright red color, the color of fresh blood. His blood?

Kachem opened the door wide and motioned Dorn inside.

Kamil hesitated a split second.

The interior of the car illuminated and Dorn recognized one of its two occupants.

Mark Lukatme was the Assistant Secretary in charge of the CIFA affairs, a lean man with quaffed raven-black hair and bleached teeth, which he liked to expose in a permanent grin of self-importance. He was of the rare breed who glided through life effortlessly. People such as Lukatme, regardless of their background, education, or social status always floated on top, alongside the top reaches of their peers, barely touching the surface of the river of life that formed a tough current for the rest. He was facing a man with a wind-beaten face of a Southerner. On the lap of the stranger was an 8x10 service photograph of PFC Kamil Dorn. The Southerner's intense black eyes were piercing every nerve on Dorn's face as he entered the vehicle following a nudge from Kachem.

"Speak of the devil," said the stranger.

His guttural, heavily accented language, sent shivers down Dorn's spine, and caused his grip to tighten around the small electromagnetic field generator he kept in his pocket. The accent was unmistakable. The man was from the very place Dorn volunteered to deliver the digital drive to. Was it a coincidence to face the man on the same night Karin Platt was arrested and Dorn's contact was abducted by killers? Coincidence did not exist in the world of espionage, and Dorn clenched his jaws in preparation for the worst. He planned it so as to squeeze the trigger simultaneously with the crashing of the faux tooth containing the small but deadly capsule. He was tense in the extreme, and ready to ignite at any moment.

"Pvt. Dorn, you were brought here in this conspiratorial manner because there is a mole inside the Building," The Assistant Secretary opened without much ado. "Four hours ago the security detained an officer who's been passing highly sensitive information to the enemy. The tragedy of the situation is the more vivid for the perpetrator is none other than Capt. Karin Platt, the daughter of the late Gen. Vincent Platt. Worse still, Karin Platt worked over at DISS." He turned to the Latino and explained the acronym, "Defense Intelligence Sharing System is a high-level source of intel distributed among strategic branches."

A short hiss over Dorn's shoulder was ice-cold. Maj. Kachem was breathing heavily.

"It's alright, Mr. Kachem, we are not disclosing any secrets. The existence of DISS is known to our guest."

The stranger said nothing, only his short mustache twitched barely perceptibly.

Dorn was taken aback. *Mr.* Kachem? All kinds of rumors circulated about Maj. Will Kachem, including one, which placed him on the civilian side of the intelligence world. Many of the junior officers oft repeated it, and Kachem's own mysterious past played into the rumor. Those who believed it were generally of the troubling opinion that one Will Kachem was not an officer at all, certainly not of any known formation, but someone akin to an ideological commissar, not unlike those who once served in the Communist Block. Dorn observed Kachem those last five months, and became convinced the rumors were ingeniously planted, as was the C-*KGB*-IFA contraction, probably by Kachem himself, all in an effort to intimidate and put his prey off its stride. Now, this pompous politician seemed to confirm the rumor as fact. Was it a part of a game to throw Dorn off guard, to solicit a confession, a dagger driven into his ribs?

7. MICE

Mark Lukatme looked down on Dorn.

"I assume you are aware of the basics of espionage and counterespionage, Pvt. Dorn?"

"Dorn graduated the Fort with flying colors," Kachem volunteered when no reply was given.

The Assistant Secretary was not convinced, the young Private's silence puzzling.

He pried, "Then we don't need to go into details of Karin Platt's motivations?"

This time Kachem showed concern when his subordinate remained speechless.

"MICE, Dorn?"

"Money. Ideology. Compromise. Ego." Dorn replied mechanically.

"The most common reasons people betray," Lukatme nodded appreciatively. "No one is born a traitor, but everyone can become one given the right conditions. The acronym sums up most traitors' motivations. Platt's motivation was, arguably, the most common of them all. She did it for money."

Why do they not come to the point? Dorn thought. Go ahead, a voice shouted in his head, ask me for my motivations!

Lukatme went on, "The damage caused by Platt is incalculable, though she betrayed her country for a mere three thousand dollars a month. Pittance."

"Traitors for money are the lowest scum, Dorn," Kachem hissed.

Here we go, Dorn thought. They want to know my motivation. Why? To choose the best approach, a line of questioning. Oh, no! He won't make it as easy!

He summoned all his courage and said, "Not everything is black and white. Espionage, much as life, is composed of shades of grey."

Lukatme raised his eyebrows. He turned to Kachem, and said, "He's good." Then to Dorn, "You're right. Quite often one could stop traitors before they betray if only one took the effort to better understand them and their condition in life, alas it is not how our vetting system works." He exchanged looks with Kachem, as though seeking silent confirmation, and added in a voice not devoid of compassion, "Karin Platt indeed found herself in unenviable circumstances. An orphan, and a single mother with no money of her own, she slipped through the cracks because of that old fool with a soft heart, Col. Clooles, who took pity on her and brought her under his wing. Unfortunately, she was already turned by then."

"The question is, Dorn, who she worked with?" Kachem did not like where the conversation was leading. He was not a man to take pity. "The Building is and will remain at the core of our enemies' interest. No spy works alone. I have a gut feeling Platt's capture is only the beginning. How many Karin Platts are we dealing with?" he finished with an ominous gaze into Dorn's eyes.

Dorn could feel his face turn pale. He hoped the dim light of the interior covered the change, and in order to draw attention away, he asked, "Has Platt lead us to her control?"

"We'll come back to Platt's control in due course. First thing is to expose the other traitor." Kachem gazed at Dorn with an evanescent grin in the corner of his lips.

Not knowing how to respond to what he thought of as an outright attack, Dorn asked naïvely, "The other traitor?"

"A cutout, Dorn. The one who picked up dead drops from Platt, and carried them out of the Building. "You wanna know who?" Kachem jabbed his index finger into Dorn's chest. "Someone not invulnerable to making mistakes."

"What was the mistake?" Dorn muttered.

"It was in the nature of the material Platt stole from her boss. It's of so narrow an interest that in turn it allows us to narrow down the probable culprit."

All hair stood up on Dorn's neck. Three pairs of eyes were focused on his face. He put all the strength he could muster into his words.

"What was she after?"

This time it was the southerner who replied. His English, though accented, was clear and legible.

"The material stolen today could have dire consequences for the Superpower, when it could've and should've been used to destroy your country's worst enemy."

"The worst?" Dorn found strength in the stranger's ominous statement.

"Señor Manuel Arena flew in especially to assist us in tracking down the bastards who did this." Lukatme introduced the Latino. "And it is because of him that you are here, Pvt. Dorn."

Dorn swallowed hard. He said nothing.

The southerner said, "You served in Rome, yes?"

"Briefly," Dorn confirmed.

"Enough, I trust, to grasp the sensitive nature of the relationship between your country and the Holy See?"

A nod.

"You've also learned of the complicated network of lay and religious groups that form the backbone of the Church?" Receiving a confirmatory nod, he went on, "And you are aware that one of these groups has gone astray, and is the subject of growing concerns of the combined forces of your Defense Department, and the Holy See's Dottrina?"

Dorn sat as though on pins.

The stranger took the lack of answer for perplexity.

"Dottrina is, of course, the body responsible for the defense of the Doctrine of the Church."

"I know what it is," Dorn replied quietly. "A successor to the Inquisition."

"Perhaps the Church ought to have stayed with the name, so as to discourage dissent and treason. It had an unmatched cache."

"And what is it that concerns the Inquisition?" Dorn asked with sudden boldness, as though all cards were on the table.

"The Company."

"The Company?"

"The Company."

8. The Dossiers

Silence filled the still air inside the vehicle.

The Assistant Secretary was the first to break it.

"It's gotten hot in here."

He reached for the switch that opened the electrically operated window, and let fresh air inside. He turned to the Latino.

"Señor Arena? Why don't we come to the point?"

The windblown man gathered his thoughts before continuing in a voice, which resembled a storyteller telling tales of bogyman to children gathered around a campfire.

"We are dealing with the most serious threat to our way of life since the Bolshevik revolution—"

"Bigger!" Lukatme added.

"Such an argument has certainly been made by your very own military intelligence," Arena nodded. "And the assertion is unfounded. Bolsheviks took power with an iron fist, for the most part without the blessing of the masses. What we have now is different, worse by the order of tenfold. We are dealing with force, which is not merely ideologically driven, but powered by faith."

Sensing the foreigner was readying for a long tirade, Lukatme shot a telling glance at the illuminated face of his designer watch, and said, "Our society's infatuation with religion is to blame. We have more denominations in our country than exist in the rest of the world. But the one, which concerns us the most, is none other than the Company of Jesus."

Overwhelmed by events of the evening, Dorn did not react as the gravity of the announcement would suggest. He sat straight, his eyes glancing about the interior of limousine, resting on no place in particular.

"The Jesuits, Dorn. Our archenemy." Kachem hissed into his ear.

"Yes," Dorn muttered.

"They've gone rogue," said Arena.

"Rogue?" Dorn continued in the same way, puzzled on the surface.

"It was a gradual change," the Latino went on, "fomenting slowly, under the surface, over several decades, until it received a boost from the liberals at the Second Vatican Council. You mustn't think the Holy See was blind, far from it, and successive Popes since Paul VI took active steps to keep an eye on, even to combat, the schism. All to no avail."

"Combat? How?"

"Beginning with the dossiers. Paul VI started a detailed filing system on the Jesuits and their sympathizers. It led the Dottrina to uncover a devilish plot that threatened shatter the foundations of the Church. Are you familiar with the Fourth Vow, Private? No? Very few laypeople are. The Fourth Vow is unique to the Company. You see, in addition to the three standard vows of poverty, chastity, and obedience, the Fourth professes special obedience to the Holy Father. Not every Jesuit takes the Fourth, and those who do are the elite, the professed. Traditionally they were the backbone of every Pope, his foot soldiers. Their unwavering support saved many a Pope at times of tumult. Not anymore. The Fourth Vow or not, the Jesuits will use every skill, and every tool at their disposal to dig holes under the One they owe obedience to. They teach, preach, and advocate Gospel so fundamentally at odds with the official Doctrine that they have become the cancer that eats the Church, and may bring about its fall. In a typical example of casuistry, they claim the Fourth Vow is superceded with the Fourth Decree!"

"The what?"

"Oh, this is where they show their true, Satanic, provenance. The Jesuit conspirators convened a congregation and came up with a new decree, or an amendment to their constitution. They call it the Fourth Decree."

"Do not laugh, Private," Lukatme caught the smirk on Dorn's lips. "This is no joke. It is serious, something we haven't seen since the October Revolution. Decree Four, or the Jesuit's new gospel, or constitution, is nothing short of a call for a worldwide uprising, not unlike the one preached by the Internationale. The priests want to put an end to, as they call it — the unjust distribution of wealth and resources. They fight to bring down the established political systems. They set up their own banking systems of microloans for individuals as well as communities, and their wealth is such that it threatens the existing banking establishments. They finance bigger projects, too, competing with multinational construction and production industries. Hell, they even sponsor movements to sabotage the military-industrial complex, to say nothing of what they do to the educational system. It is a part of a well-coordinated machination under the banner to transform the world's structures in the interest of material liberation of the peoples, and you know what similar calls led to in 1917 Russia, and later in Cuba—"

Dorn could not help another grin.

"Mr. Secretary is correct. One must not underestimate the danger the Jesuits presents to the world at large," the foreigner took up the subject. "When we took down Che, we thought we killed the idea. We were wrong. His death passed the torch of uprising on to the priests."

Such blatant vilification of the Company fuelled Dorn's inherent courage. He wanted to argue, to put himself in the shoes of the Fathers, the missionaries who devoted their lives to spreading the Word, to enlightening those who knew no better — to converting the enemies of the Company and the New Church. Perhaps he would have entered into an argument were it not for the tingling sensation in the back of his neck.

Feeling Kachem's fangs inch closer and closer, he said with subdued anger, "What are you suggesting, Mr. Arena? That the Jesuits changed allegiance? To whom? The Prince of Darkness?"

The foreigner's two glowing embers intensified as they focused on Dorn's face.

"You're not far off, Private. The Jesuits's transformation from the Pope's men into radical revolutionaries has forced the priests underground. Perhaps not in the Biblical sense, but in a militant way. Many of the Fathers defrocked in order to join the Invisible Company, the underground movement whose purpose is to protect and to preserve the Order, whatever the cost to the Church at large—"

Dorn could not help but snicker. He said nothing, but his face expressed what words did not.

"Did I say something funny?" Arena asked.

Dorn checked himself, and replied in a conciliatory tone, "Rather unbelievable."

"Unbelievable is their audacity! Together they fight for the abolition of the priestly character of their order, and openly oppose Church Hierarchy, even going as far as demanding the abdication of the Holy Father! None of it, however, is as grievous as their opposition to the Dogma. They knock the bottom out of the Immaculate Conception and Assumption of the Virgin. They ridicule the Seven Sacraments, and apply pseudo-scientific criticism to the scriptures, not to mention such daily headline darlings as the advocacy for the use of contraceptives, acceptance of homosexuality, abortion, and the abolishing of celibacy—"

"These are grave sins, indeed!" Dorn said coldly, but carefully. The vehemence of Arena's words was of a peculiar nature, almost personal, and it told him to remain on his guard.

"Señor Arena is a member of the Opus Dei," Lukatme chimed in when prolonged silence showed no signs of easing.

Dorn inhaled deeply. Opus Dei. Of course! The Jesuits' arch enemy.

It was time to lay down the gloves.

He took another breath, and said, "Forgive me, Mr. Secretary, but why do these internal Church squabbles concern the government?"

"This is the crux of the matter, Pvt. Dorn. The Company's activities are not only aimed at the Holy See, but also against our country. On the face of it their struggle is directed at the antiquated Church, but their actions endanger the very fabric of our society. The Jesuits — the scientists, the teachers, and the theologians — who, for so many decades, educated our youth, who reaped the rewards of living in a free and democratic society, and in relative autonomy from the Holy See, have blindly embraced the most dangerous thought of our time." Lukatme paused for effect, and finished in a theatrically dramatic tone, "The Liberation Theology."

9. The Manifesto

Dorn did not reply immediately. His eyes traveled from one face to another, until, suddenly, he realized why he was brought here, to this secluded location, to a meeting meant to remain hidden from official scrutiny. These men did not bring him here to crucify. He was certain of it now, for they would not have engaged in as long and convoluted an attempt to extract his confession. Maj. Kachem knew far better ways to convince his prey to talk than engage in a cheap play. It could only mean that something else was afoot. What? He would have to balance on a fine thread to find out without giving away his secret. It occurred to him that playing a dilettante may get him further than going on a defensive. But controlled dilettantism it would be.

"The Liberation Theology?" Dorn repeated after the Assistant Secretary.

Lukatme snorted, and ejaculated, "A noble and Christian concept abused and manipulated by demagogues as means to succeed where the Bolsheviks failed!" He checked himself and continued more composedly, "It isn't just rhetoric they preach. The Jesuits took to Liberation Theology to overthrow our way of life. They actually take to the streets along with the unions and socialists. They lobby for business-restrictive labor laws, and nationalization of industries. Ask them what they believe in and they will say: Christian Democratic Socialism. Well, *Democratic* my ass! It's Christian communism!"

With his glowing eyes he turned to the foreigner, and finished, "'Scuse my latin."

Gathering his thoughts, Manuel Arena tapped on Dorn's service photograph, and said to the beat of his finger, "The Jesuits engage in a dangerous ideology based on deliberately false interpretation of the Holy Scriptures. They use the verses 44 and 45 of chapter 2 of the Acts of the Apostles to call the masses to arms, and they must be stopped in a like way!"

"Ay," cheered the Assistant Secretary, and gazed to Dorn.

"I'm not familiar with the Bible," said Dorn.

The foreigner snorted.

"To understand the enemy is to beat him at his game."

His eyes suddenly narrow, he raised his head, and quoted, *"And all that believed were together, and had all things common. And sold their possessions and goods, and parted them to all men, as every man had need."*

If the quotation was intended to solicit a reply, it failed. Dorn's face remained blank. Silence lasted at least a minute. It was broken by Lukatme.

"As you see the Company uses the Bible as a sort of… Marxist Manifesto."

Arena nodded in confirmation.

"It resonates with the masses. And it appeals to an ever-growing number of religious Orders, including the Franciscans. If not stopped it will consume the Church altogether."

Dorn loosened his collar — an instinctive and innocuous gesture caused by the heated interior, but one which his opponents could take for a sign of discomfort of a different nature. To cover the gesture he raised his voice, "Is it not in the Church's power to stop the Company?"

"The tragedy of it is that the Company is the Church. Its voice is perceived as the voice of the Church. Its networks built over the centuries reach untold millions. It has followers in every corner of the world, in every sector of public life. The Jesuits not only spread contraceptives and advocate planned parenthood, but they lead organized labor and professional organizations, they command civil servants, as well as lobby groups, guerillas, militaries, and public institutions, including educational ones. Together they advocate— no! not simply advocate, but fight for such dangerous causes as abolition of social classes, private property, and State—" the Latino stopped to catch his breath. He was panting, small drops glistened at his temples.

Lukatme took over.

"The upshot of it is, that the Company has become undesirable within the Church and in our country."

Dorn's only reply was a questioning look.

The Assistant Secretary clarified, "We mustn't permit the cancer to spread onto our soil, and into the minds of our domestic Catholics."

Dorn's face retained the perplexed appearance.

Arena addressed Lukatme with reproach, "You assured me you've chosen the right man."

Lukatme looked to Kachem in turn.

The Major's icy breath gripped Dorn's neck when he said, "Dorn is the right man. He'll do it. He'll deliver the deadly blow to the Company."

10. Trojan Horse

Dorn could not help it. A single word had slipped out from under his stupefied breath.

"What?"

Señor Arena said, "The opportunity to deliver a decisive blow to the Company slipped by our predecessors' fingers during Paul VI's reign. It is why we now must use means appropriate for dealing with terrorists."

"Terrorists?"

"Make no mistake, Private. The Company of today is a terrorist organization."

This was too much for Dorn. He thought he had heard everything by now. From starting Masonic lodges, plotting to overthrow governments, murdering monarchs, and inciting wars, to causing global financial catastrophes, and poisoning the Popes, the Company's five-hundred year history has been the subject of countless conspiracy theories, none as outrageous as the one presented to Dorn today. Yet a quick glance into the Southerner's eyes convinced Dorn the calumny was considered seriously.

"Terrorists?" he repeated, still unable to come to terms with the outrageous accusation.

The Assistant Secretary amplified, bending a manicured finger for each example used to support the assertion, "Training guerillas to blow up military installations and infrastructures, orchestrating campaigns to undermine governments, conducting sabotage to destabilize economies — The whole works! Revolutionaries. Extremists. Insurgents. Terrorists. Jesuits. Same devil. Their names may be many, but their aim is only one — to demolish the foundations of the free world."

Dorn was speechless. Unable to offer counter-arguments in the face of this blatantly hateful attack, he muttered, "How— How am I to stop it?"

Mark Lukatme said, "We must balance as carefully as if we were on the edge of a razor. With the Company's deep entrenchment in our society, our plans, if failed, could lead to a major blowback." He turned to Kachem. "Perhaps we ought to catch Karin Platt's accomplice first, to ensure the files did not reach the enemy—"

"It's only a matter of time," Kachem assured, while his hand, as though by accident, brushed by Dorn's.

They did not know. Kachem might suspect Dorn, and God knows what fueled his suspicions, but he has no proof! Encouraged by the realization, Dorn asked, "Do we suspect anyone?"

"*We* suspect everyone, Dorn. But in this case it isn't about what we suspect, but what we know."

"We do?"

"We know where and how the exchange will take place, thus the evolution is as follows—"

"The evolution?" the Opus Dei representative pricked his ear.

"Plan of the operation," Kachem explained the military term.

In those four words Maj. Kachem showed contempt for the foreign civilian. Kachem did not hide contempt for anyone.

"Which is?" Dorn asked.

"The Company dispatched a courier to pick up the goods stolen by Karin Platt. We shall allow the exchange to take place, only the courier shall receive what we want him to carry back to the Company's headquarters."

"A Trojan Horse?"

Two eyes focused on Dorn's. Those were the eyes of the engineer of the devilish plan aimed to implode the Company from within.

"You'll learn the specifics in due course," Kachem said.

The Assistant Secretary added, "Your mission is to find and stop the mole who picked up the dead drop."

"And the Trojan Horse?"

"Then the courier will carry a prepared device to the Company headquarters—"

"What's in it?" Dorn's fingers pat the package in his pocket.

"You are not cleared for such details, Private!" Lukatme said scornfully.

"How am I to succeed if I'm kept in the dark?"

"Failure is not an option!" Kachem spat out. He reached to the seat next to the Assistant Secretary, and picked up a manila envelope. He extracted a black-and-white drawing, glanced at it briefly, and passed it on to Dorn. "The mission is threefold. To deliver a package to the courier, to find Platt's accomplice, and this man."

With his heart at his throat Dorn studied the familiar face. The likeness was uncanny, though drawn by a sketch artist. Looking considerably older, a wide bruised forehead above a set of peaceful eyes of undetermined color, and a grandfatherly smile, this was the face of his friend and mentor.

"Karin Platt's recruiter." Kachem watched closely for the effect made by the announcement.

Dorn studied the sketch with feigned indifference. The likeness was a remarkable accomplishment considering its bearer possessed the sort of countenance, which made him indistinguishable in the crowd. Karin Platt's ability to describe him, despite having met only once, a long time ago, spoke to her keen eye and attention to detail. Without raising his head he gazed to the manila envelope wondering what other surprises it contained.

"We were able to match the man with another case." Kachem drew out a second sheet from the envelope.

Staring from the page was the same man, though at east two decades younger.

The Major continued, "This sketch was obtained by the Opus Dei, drawn on site by their numeral who infiltrated a Jesuit meeting."

Manuel Arena added, "The man is one of the Company's most accomplished covert agents. He's been known to have recruited countless military officers in my country, as well as yours."

Dorn swallowed hard.

"What am I to do?" he asked in a trembling voice.

"Curb your enthusiasm," Kachem apparently misconstrued Dorn's reaction. "Death is something he will pray for when I lay my hands on him..."

11. Last Temptation

Maj. Kachem gave a briefing on the objectives of the mission. It raised more questions than offered answers. Dorn understood only that he would leave immediately to the hotbed of the Company's struggle. He understood that he would be working under an assumed identity. It was the latter, the necessity to furnish him with a false persona, that delayed the departure, and presented him with an opportunity to pass on a coded message.

Upon return to the Building, waiting for his new papers, Dorn sought a secure terminal, one exempt from the all-seeing eyes and all-hearing ears of the No-Such-Agency. Such terminals were made available as part of the military's increased role in intelligence gathering and processing. Nonetheless, using such a terminal to send a coded message to a Jesuit recipient came with great risk. Alas, Dorn could not help it. He was out of options, and found hope in the secure code used by the Company's field agents. He would have preferred to use the never broken, official code, however, if traced to him, it would undoubtedly peg him as a Jesuit agent. Thus, instead, he opted for the oft used Nahuatl derivative, which functioned to great success among agents operating in the field, and was used by all sides involved in the conflict. The code was not without its pitfalls, though, its use decreasing due to complexity. Ideographic in its entirety, the Nahuatl code was simple and secure, alas often misinterpreted due to varying regional specifics. Its cryptographic strength was chiefly in its free interpretation, which was also its biggest weakness, and led to gradual departure from the code. Both the sender and the recipient required common understanding of not only the pictographs, but more importantly of the idea they represented, hence shared cultural background, or ideology, were of paramount importance. Dorn counted on shared interests, passions, friendship, and goals when dispatching the message, and returned to his office with mixed feelings, uncertainty prevailing and dominating all other thoughts.

"Wanna see the dead drop?"

The voice startled him. Maj. Kachem had the propensity for sneaking up on people. Unseen, unheard, and unexpected, he appeared out of nowhere, unsettling his prey. This time was no different. Dorn would have jumped up had he been seated. Instead he stopped abruptly, and took an instinctive step back, which was interpreted as an agreement.

Kachem led the way, choosing the same route Dorn followed whenever a drop was scheduled. Dorn studied it carefully before he settled on it. It was neither a direct nor the most convenient way. With several possible ways to approach the marble planter, he spent time picking one which showed his back to the closed-circuit cameras located in the vicinity of the staircase. As though taunting him, Kachem did the same. Dorn put on a brave face. He reasoned that, when confronted, he picked the route on his first day and stuck to it out of habit. It was not an unreasonable line of defense, given the Building was an immense structure, employing some 30,000 people who trotted its 50,000 miles of corridors. Dorn convinced himself that in the end Kachem had no reason to suspect him, and the Major's actions were the result of his ingrained suspicious nature.

It became apparent that Maj. Kachem did not choose the route by coincidence. To reach the staircase they had to take a sharp turn. Like Satan setting up the last temptation, Kachem stopped abruptly, without indicating the destination, and allowed Dorn to pass him and lead the way. The provocation, though clear, was played out masterfully, and Dorn would have perhaps succumbed were it not for two officers who at the same time appeared from around the corner. Bumping into them, Dorn stopped in his tracks, realizing belatedly what was at play.

A barely perceptible grin contorted the Major's lips before he carried on.

Recounting the devious nature of his superior officer, Dorn soon faced a test more challenging. With the staircase ahead of them, he could see men and women descending, with others climbing. The latter appeared above the level of the floor slowly, their heads first, followed by torsos. Dorn's eyes followed them absentmindedly until his eyes caught a familiar face. Karin Platt was heading toward him, followed by a security detail. She walked lightly, as though a heavy load was taken off her shoulders — a sensation common among fugitives when finally caught, their uncertain condition resolved. Dorn noticed the sudden change on the woman's face, and her posture, as her eyes rested on him. She recognized him. How? He could not tell, but it was clear that she must have spotted him at one time or another as he picked up the caches she delivered. With his heart in his throat he marched on, his legs turned to jelly. He continued on under the spell of her eyes, nearing on a deadly collision, unable to turn away, as a prey hypnotized by a snake.

Time stood still when they passed, their arms brushing, the air molecules, which surrounded each, mixing together. It was during the brief physical contact when Dorn realized the paralyzing emotions, while shared by the woman, were not caused by him, but rather by his companion, the man who arrested and interrogated her.

The confrontation did not work out as Maj. Kachem had hoped. Dorn felt the heavy sigh of disappointment, as the officer breathed on his neck, but dared not glance into the face lest his own betray him. He broke into cold sweat but could not bring himself to wipe it off his forehead. He had passed the challenge, albeit with his legs trembling at his knees. He was afraid to tumble down the stairs. Every step he took felt as though he was entering a void.

To his relief, Maj. Kachem stopped in front of the familiar marble planter without conducting additional tests.

"That it?" Dorn asked.

"Pretty darn-in-your-face simple," Kachem replied with his squinted eyes set on Dorn's. He added, "Can you find it?"

Dorn hesitated.

"Don't worry, we've lifted fingerprints already."

Kachem had not given up his suspicions, and Dorn knew he would not until the mole was found. Confident that no concrete evidence existed, else the Major would not subject him to these tests, he set out to perform as best he could. And as performance it was worthy of a theatrical stage. Dorn circled around the planter, examining it visually from all angles, feeling the underneath, the edges, and finally reached into to the dark crevice between the marble and the plastic drainage tank.

"Bra-vo!" Kachem hissed with sultry pleasure.

12. Hollie Weader

The drive to the airport was a breeze at this early hour, yet it dragged on mercilessly for Dorn. Maj. Kachem's silence was the more ominous for the unspoken. How much did the Major know? How much of the unsaid was simply the result of his suspicious nature? How many more tests awaited ahead? To better face them Dorn had to learn more about his mission.

"Am I to receive support?" he asked when they pulled in to the departure's drop-off area.

Kachem extracted a large envelope from his briefcase.

"Everything you need to know is here."

Dorn shook the contents out, and studied them.

"Any of our people on site?"

"You'll contact Chad Fink, a snitch for the Opus Dei. Despite his seemingly menial job, he is very well connected, and knows all you need to carry out your mission." He then explained how to contact the said man.

"And is he my entire support?"

"It is imperative to keep a low profile, Dorn. Remember the country is a major center of the Company's operations."

"What about the embassy?"

"Out of the question. This op is strictly off the books."

Kachem added after brief silence, "Anything you and Weader may need on site, you will receive from Fink."

"Weader?"

"Capt. Weader."

"The Capt. Weader?" Dorn was taken aback.

"The very one. Undoubtedly it's a privilege, Dorn. Not many can boast of having worked with Capt. Weader. But don't let it go to your head. The two of you have separate missions, and Weader's objectives are dictated by the DSS."

"Ought this even be a joint mission, then?"

"Don't be dramatic."

"But the DSS—"

"The DSS and the CIFA both have their place. A bit of competition in intelligence gathering is good for the country," Kachem replied diplomatically.

"And keeping tabs on one another?"

He hit Kachem's sore spot. Pitching various services against its rivals was the best guarantor of any regime's survival. Nowhere was this rivalry stronger than between the Defense Security Service and the CIFA. Maj. Kachem believed, however, that the CIFA was better suited for the purpose of ensuring ideological unity across the land. His efforts equaled only those of the legendary Capt. Weader's of the DSS, and Dorn could not help the feeling that he has found himself between the proverbial rock and a hard place.

Both accomplished spycatchers, their tactics differed somewhat. Kachem preferred a direct and open approach, signaling his prey about an imminent attack, thus instilling fear, which often led to mistakes and capture, whereas Capt. Weader favored a low profile, striking suddenly and with the precision of a night owl. For all intents and purposes Weader was exactly that — unseen, and unheard — a night owl. Very few had ever met the accomplished officer, whose successes were synonymous with the name. Many believed that the Capt. Weader of the legends did not exist at all, and was only that — a myth created by the service to the same effect Kachem's overwhelming presence had often achieved — to instill fear and uncertainty where the seed of treason might find fertile ground. Now, as Dorn was about to find out, the legend was in fact very real.

"Your assignment, Dorn, is something many guys would trade a lot for. Succeed, and promotion is a given; fail and you'll dream of Capt. Weader from a deep dungeon."

A sudden loathsomeness on Kachem's face was explained by the most unexpected sight.

The mysterious, often feared, and legendary Capt. Weader's first name was… Hollie.

The tall and lithe brunette with a short but wide forehead, a lightly snubbed nose, and voluptuous lips, was in fact an attractive woman. Light carry-on luggage, casual hikers, and a matching dress presented an image of a typical tourist en route to a southern holiday destination, but a tanned face suggested a return rather than a departure.

"The red eye did not impede your beauty, Captain," Kachem opened with a wide smile, in a tone suggesting familiarity.

"What have I done wrong not to earn a first-class seat?" she retorted while waiving a printed ticket in her hand.

"We wouldn't want you to soften out," Kachem went on jovially.

A smile wider than his lipless face could, seemingly, project, was a peculiar sight, not becoming of the somber, almost cruel looking officer. It did not take big observational skills to realize that Kachem was infatuated with the attractive officer.

Dorn was fascinated with the discovery and did not know whether to keep his eyes on his superior officer, or the ravishing brunette, when he froze suddenly. With the corner of his eye he caught a face he was worried he would never see again. He turned pale. With Kachem chattering loquaciously, in a style unbecoming his persona, Dorn hoped his reaction went unnoticed.

It did not escape Capt. Weader's penetrating eyes. She was used to evoking a considerably different reaction from men whose path she crossed. This young agent seemed uninterested in her, and it intrigued her. As she picked a large envelope from Kachem and listened to his briefing, her eyes followed the man she was partnered with. He grew increasingly discomforted. His eyes, while glimpsing from her to Kachem, lacked focus — they were not seeing what they were glancing, they were looking through, not at. She followed Dorn's gaze.

"First time in the field?" she asked.

He offered an unclear reply, something between a grunt and a sigh.

"Your reputation precedes you," Kachem suggested, and diverted Weader's attention with a continual chatter. Had he followed Dorn's gaze he would have noticed an older gentleman whose face bore an uncanny likeness to a sketch he was passing on to Capt. Weader at the very moment.

13. Handsome and Honeypot

It was not until they had boarded and the airplane took off that Dorn was able to breathe a sigh of relief. The flight was not nearly sold out, with numerous empty seats scattered around the cabin. With a row to themselves the two officers were able to conduct an uninterrupted and fairly private conversation.

"Will mentioned you have had prior experience with the Church," Capt. Hollie Weader started.

"Exaggeration. Just a tour of duty in Rome," Dorn replied, his eyes scanning the cabin for the familiar face.

"Clearly it's much more if you were picked for this op."

"Frankly, I don't know why Maj. Kachem—"

"No rank!"

"Yes, Capt.— Hollie. I don't know why Will picked me."

"I'm no longer Hollie, remember?" she said, frustrated with his wondering mind. "Any field experience?"

Dorn did not reply immediately. A man stood up from his seat several rows in front of them, and began a slow trek

51

to the back of the aircraft. Dorn's chin drooped, but quickly rose again in alarm. He looked into the woman's lagoon eyes, and replied in order to draw her attention away from the approaching man, "Mostly desk, which is why I don't understand why I'm here, next to someone like you."

"Like me?"

"You're a legend."

"It didn't happen overnight, you know."

"What's your secret?"

"I've witnessed plenty of good agents burned, not because they lacked skill, or knowledge, but simply because they underestimated their opponent."

"I do not underestimate our opponents, if that's what you worry about."

She looked him up and down.

"No, you don't look like you would."

"But you think my experience, or lack thereof, poses a risk."

"I admit the thought crossed my mind. But a fresh face is not necessarily a bad thing, if you consider the Jesuits have a long collective memory." She studied his face for some time, and added, "You're handsome, in… trust evoking sort of way. You may do well in field, provided you're a good actor. Are you?"

"I hope so."

"I bet you are."

He caught irony in her voice, and thought it better to say nothing.

"I bet you are," she went on, "or else you're withholding something. I don't like secrets, not where they affect my safety and impede the success of the operation."

"Did Will not share my service record?"

"Service records be damned! To survive in this field you need something else. Calling. Do you have a calling?"

He looked deeply into her eyes, and said with honesty, "Calling is the reason I'm doing it."

She studied him closely, with intensity, her gaze burrowing deep under his skull. Suddenly the crease between her brows smoothed, and she smiled.

"Good."

"What is your calling?" he parried to keep her talking.

"You mean — what is a woman doing in a man's world?"

She said it so seriously Dorn could not help but smile.

"I'm not that chauvinist, though one can't help but wonder why pick a female agent to break a male religious order?"

"Where the devil can't reach he'll send a woman," she replied with a smile. "I'm not a *honeypot*, though. It wouldn't work with these men, anyway—"

"You're *handsome* enough to wonder otherwise."

She looked at him, and burst out laughing.

"I see what you mean. It was unfair of me to insinuate that you would do well in the field because of your physical features. They aren't everything, but the reality is they are an important bonus."

"This why the DSS chose a female agent?"

"Perhaps it was a twofold decision. Our opponents don't expect a woman to try to infiltrate their Order, since their chastity is legendary. At the same time a woman can evoke certain trust, though not only because she is not expected to pose a deadly risk, but for more human reasons. Call it longing, perhaps."

This woman represented the deadliest enemy who fought the Company directly and by proxy wars, yet Dorn could not help but smile again. Something about Hollie Weader was utterly disarming and the realization of it brought his smile to end just as quickly as it appeared. He sensed a troubled road ahead.

"Your results prove that a woman can do the same job, and better," he said sincerely.

"Tell it to Will."

"Oh? I would've thought him rather— impressed. He even said something to the effect that he was envious of your successes."

"I'll bet he is. It's an important assignment."

"Are you and Will well acquainted?"

"You mean — since before the uniform?"

"It's hard to imagine Maj. Kachem without a uniform."

"Major?" She snorted and appeared ready to burst out laughing. "I meant — since before my uniform. But since you mentioned it, Will may wear a uniform, but he sure as hell never attended any military academy."

Dorn's ears pricked up. He was genuinely surprised.

"He was my instructor at the intelligence school," he said. "Which course?"

"Resistance to Interrogation."

"Lemme guess — the part of the R2I involving the prolonged nakedness and sexual humiliation?"

Dorn laughed.

"Among others. Attended by most male instructors whenever female students were present."

* * *

The meals were served and the trays were cleared before Dorn found the opportunity to excuse himself. Offering to procure drinks he pushed by the line up which formed to the lavatories, and entered the pantry at the tail section. He picked up two plastic cups, and waited his turn to the water bottles.

An elderly man of silver hair, the only other person present in the pantry, took his time to fiddle with a bottle cap. He said over his shoulder, without facing Dorn, "I always knew you were the right person for the mission. How did you ever convince them of your innocence?"

"I didn't," Dorn replied under his nose. "I think they do suspect me."

The elderly man's shoulders stiffened. He filled his cup, and passed the bottle.

"They have proof?" he asked with his lips over the rim of his cup.

"They are fishing for one."

"What is your situation?"

Dorn filled his cup and drank the contents in one long swig. He poured again and, mimicking the man, he spoke with his lips around the rim of the plastic cup.

"They are using me to get to the courier."

"We shall be prepared."

"Brother Anselm—" Dorn bit his tongue. "I think it is time to expect the worse."

"How so?"

"They are convinced they can bring down the Company. I admit, I am worried. After centuries of persecutions we may have found an enemy capable of delivering the final blow."

"They can't succeed now that we know about an imminent attack."

"They can if the woman I'm traveling with is successful."

"Who is she?"

Dorn explained the rivalry between the two agencies involved, and of the unknown objectives of Capt. Weader.

He finished with, "She is bad news. She's traveling as Karin Platt, with a delivery for the courier."

"What is it?"

"Kachem seems convinced it's a Trojan Horse."

"Then we must stop her, mustn't we?"

"We must, but it won't be easy. They are watching me, I can feel it. Kachem wants Platt's accomplice. One false move and I'm done."

"They won't find him. Not in you. You're too smart."

"You don't know Maj. Will Kachem. He wants the accomplice. He'll get him. If he doesn't, then Capt. Hollie Weader will."

They fell silent for a time, sipping from their cups.

"She can make you out," Dorn said. "Platt provided your sketch, which was matched with another obtained from Opus Dei."

They could not help it. Their eyes ventured over the rows and to the woman in question. She was standing in the alley, ostensibly to procure something from her carry on luggage, her face turned toward them. Their eyes met.

Dorn's face turned white. He forced a smile to his lips, and said aloud and in a guilty tone, "Gracias, señor."

14. Destiny's Path

Brother Anselm's eyes followed his protégé — the younger version of himself, as he liked to think of Dorn. He observed the confidence with which Dorn carried himself, and could not help but summon the image of a terrified, guilt-stricken boy he met some years ago. He recalled the months of therapy, and the long period of convalescence comprising countless sessions with the Company's therapists, which helped reconstruct the events that led to the tragedy, and ultimately thrust the boy under his guidance...

"Mom, are we there yet?" the seven year old girl asked in a long drawl, apparently weary from repeating the same question, bored of the monotonous desert horizon.

The mother did not reply, equally tired of hearing the whining voice. The three months since her husband's passing, dealing with the estate, the move, and the kids, had drained the life fluids out of her. She had not yet had the time to mourn what with the end of the school year. As all parents she developed the ability to suppress those brain receptors responsible for processing children's cries when they only vied for attention, but this time even she grew weary of the monotonous trip and the persistent child. The malfunctioning compressor in the old clunker only added to her frustration.

"Mo-om! Kamil is showing food in his mouth!"

Only two more hours, she reminded herself. She concentrated on the arrival, the shower that awaited at the end of the journey, the air-conditioned house of her brother's, the warmth of his welcome. She tried not to venture in her thoughts beyond the immediate future where uncertainty clashed with hope. The last two months proved more than she could bear. Her brother's invitation was a godsend. She sold the house, settled what debts she could, packed what she could not part with into the wagon, and drove south. This was the beginning of the rest of her and the kids' life after John. She had not expected to pull it off this far, she never thought living without the loving and loved husband and father possible; it was necessary, for the sake of the kids, for the sake of his memory.

"Mo-o-om!"

In two hours she would rest in her brother's arms. She could really use the physical closeness, the psychological strength derived from unflinching love of the only living relative. She looked forward to the emotional rest after months of hardship that followed the unexpected death of her spouse, a friend, a lover. It was the worst three months of her life. In two short hours she would finally have quiet time to herself.

"Mo-om!"

She turned her head abruptly, in her eyes lightning that could break trees. It did not break the child, but it brought momentary silence.

The silence lasted two minutes.

"Mom, Kam is making faces at me!"

She looked into the rearview mirror. She said what she hoped would pacify the girl, "Kamil, I asked you to look *after* Sammie, not *at* her."

Kamil did not reply. He was a good boy. Even at this trying age of fifteen she could count on him to help around the house, to ease the little chores which, if unchecked, would pile into an insurmountable mess of a headache. He walked his little sister to school, helped with meals, cleaning, and shopping. He was more serious than other boys his age, at any age, always buried in books. What else was there for a boy to do in as small a place as their hamlet, but watch TV or read? Still, as mature for his age as he appeared, Kamil was a boy, and as much as he tried to appear a grown up, and to live up to the challenge of the trying time, he remained but a boy. Such as this time.

"Mom, Kam pinched my arm! It really hurts—"

Not receiving the sympathy she felt she deserved the little Sammie began to cry, not out of pain, but a tearless cry aimed at getting attention.

It was too much. The mother could not stand this for two more hours. She jerked the wheel to pull over, at the same time she tried to project her parental displeasure — she turned around to face the kids, and the move caused her to turn the wheel further than necessary. She counteracted by jerking it back, and it caused the attached trailer to fishtail. Soon the vehicle was beyond control. She struggled with the wheel but to no avail. In the side mirror she saw the trailer flip to its side, its size and weight pulling the station wagon along. The speed and weight sent the vehicle and the trailer on a carousel spin along the pavement and on the path of an oncoming tractor trailer.

When Kamil came to he was lying on the side of the dusty road. It took time before he registered the commotion and the shouts. Then came the vision. Black smoke covered the sky. He saw people running, he heard them scream but could not make out the words. He struggled to his feet. Someone tried to hold him down. It would not do — Kamil was tall and strong, made the stronger with sudden return of the memory of the event.

"Mom?"

He shook off the hands that gripped his arm and rushed toward the clump of metal and the source of the smoke.

"Mom!" he cried as loud as his lungs permitted. He felt pain in his chest. He wiped the moisture that formed at his mouth. It tasted funny. He stopped and looked at the red blotch on his hand. He felt dizzy. With his heart at his throat he moaned, "Mom— Sammie—"

He approached several bystanders who gathered in a semicircle. He looked over their shoulders to see what drew their interest. A man was bent over a little girl who lay stretched on the side of the road, performing resuscitation. Kamil could not take his eyes off of the spasms the man's actions caused to the small body, every press on the chest causing Sammie's feet to jerk. His eyes were fixed on the shoeless feet, their movement, from side to side — a pendulum hypnotizing him. No longer able to resist he gave in to the force that pulled him away from the scene. They dragged him away. The last thing he saw were a pair of scratched bare legs, part of a churned and torn skirt he recognized as that of his mother's. He did not see her face. A bystander had mercilessly covered the upper torso and the head with his jacket.

Kamil escaped the accident relatively unscathed, with only superficial physical wounds. Much deeper were the cuts to his psyche. The shock of seeing the lifeless and mutilated bodies of his loved ones, in full exposure of gruesome violence, would take a long time to lessen. The feeling of guilt for causing the accident would require extraordinary effort to heal. Every day that followed the accident that claimed the lives of his mother and sister, he relived the moments that might have been had he behaved like the responsible young man the mother saw in him. After dad's passing he was the man of the house. In his mind he was long ready for the task. Six feet tall, with a slim but strong body developed by two years of rigorous Tae-Kwon-do, sharp-eyed, astute, and mature beyond his age, Kamil felt ready for the challenge that struck the family. No longer were his household duties confined to taking out garbage and mowing the grass. He was a full-fledged member of the executive branch of the reduced family unit. He was not only expected to do the chores of the suddenly departed member but to also foresee, plan, and delegate tasks, which every adult tackled in the course of every day. Kamil was now mother's right hand, her help and mainstay on the home front. He was in charge of ensuring the house was stocked with groceries, that incoming bills were organized and readied for settlement according to importance and availability of funds, but above all he was the guardian of the little Sammie and a buffer between the fussy girl and the over-burdened mother. It was the latter that made Kamil particularly proud, for more than anything else it was the sense of responsibility for others that closest resembled adulthood.

The day of the journey south, to their new lives, he failed at that chore and he found no excuse for the way he behaved, child-like, when he was faced with what his coevals seldom had a chance to experience — adulthood. Nominally still a kid, he now had responsibilities, and he also possessed authority over his dependent. If this was not what adulthood was all about then he could not think what else it could be. He embraced it and he failed miserably. His immaturity cost his sister's and mother's lives. Having realized the cruel reality that he was no longer an adult, yet not quite a kid anymore, he did not see how he could possibly go on, how he could ever grow up.

Psychological care received after the accident did little to erase the feeling of guilt, but drugs helped suppress possible desperate steps. Ultimately, what save the boy was the uncle's loving care and guidance. The uncle's approach differed dramatically from one taken by the psychiatrists. Rather than fight the notion, which had overtaken the young and impressionable mind, rather than argue about the blame, where only an accident was at fault, the uncle saw the feeling of guilt engraved in the boy's psyche as not merely the result of the events that precipitated the accident, but as the reflection of the boy's want of redemption.

The uncle sat with Kamil, man-to-man, adult-to-adult, and laid it on the table, "If you feel responsible for the accident then so be it, but tormenting yourself, and indulging in the feeling of guilt is not a way to recompense for what happened. Taking the easy way out is not how an adult deals with mistakes. Confronting your demons, and setting things right, is what a responsible adult does."

He had the boy's attention. He succeeded where the system failed — by reaching out to a boy who wanted to be a man. The chance for salvation thus offered by an uncle, a man of unsurpassed moral standing, a priest, a man of God, was worth infinitely more than a patronizing dismissal of pill-pushing psychiatrists whose understanding of a tormented soul was reduced to attempts to suppress it. The institutionalized approach to live and forget, if only by way of drugging the troubled youth, was countered by an offer of spiritual renewal and healing. The uncle's standing within the Company helped streamline the long and strict application process, and one Spring day a novitiate welcomed a new member.

Brother Anselm remembered the day Kamil arrived at the novitiate. It was the day that forever changed the boy's destiny. It was the day that forever bound the two of them on a quest for a better world.

15. Small World

Two plastic cups in his hands, Dorn returned to his seat and froze. Capt. Weader was gazing out the window, the sketch of Brother Anselm's face on the fold out table in front of her.

Her eyes as cold as the air outside she forced a smile and accepted the cup. Dorn sensed the not so subtle change in her. The woman was charged as a magnet, and struggled to hide it.

"Friendly people, these," she said.

It took an effort equal to pulling a stubborn ass not to glance the sketch. Dorn felt his purposeful avoidance was apparent, yet it would not do, he could not set eyes on the uncanny likeness and remain straight-faced. His eyes locked with hers he smiled in return.

"Is he from there?" she asked innocently.

"What makes you think he's from there?" he replied, his voice on edge.

"We are en route to—"

"Of course," he gasped. "No— I mean— Yes— A ranchero."

She appeared not to notice his stumbling.

"*Tu hablo Español*," she said.

"As do you, I'm sure."

His mind was racing. Did she, or did she not recognize the face from the sketch?

"Spanish, Italian, Portuguese, French," she recited without bragging, merely stating a fact. And then she charged, "What were your assignments in Rome?"

Dorn was taken off guard. Baffled, he gathered his thoughts.

She read his silenced in her own way.

"You carry a whole bag of secrets."

He saw no harm in answering what she could learn through official channels.

"Raw data analysis from our field operatives in the Chaldean Christian Movement."

Her eyebrows arched.

"Syria? Wait! Iraq?" She flicked her thumb. "Good potential for career advancement. That why you were picked for this mission?"

Dorn sighed with relief. Perhaps Capt. Weader did not make the connection between the sketch and the living person, after all? Perhaps it was only Dorn's heightened perception, which made him see the resemblance?

"In this job one does not get to pick assignments," he replied almost enthusiastically.

"Aye, aye! One might even draw similarities between our work and the Jesuits'. They too follow orders, and are sent to where they are needed the most."

Doubts, like dark clouds, filled the air between them, again. Was she testing him? If so she found a worthy opponent. His spirits freshly rejuvenated, he decided to parry.

"The similarities are true only to a point. The Jesuits would say they serve a higher cause, with no regard for such temporal temptations as promotions, and comfortable retirement."

She did not budge.

He continued, determined to see into her mind, "How many of us can boast of doing our job out of some higher calling?"

She drank, and glanced to the sketch in front of her. She turned the empty cup in her fingers, and said, "We are soldiers, not missionaries."

"How can we offer a meaningful challenge to the personal conviction of being chosen to become one of His Companions?" Dorn asked with his head raised to the ceiling, his eyes penetrating beyond.

Her fingers continued to turn the cup, and her eyes remained on the penciled sketch for a time. Suddenly she turned to Dorn, and said, "Are you suggesting that our men and women in uniform do not believe in what they do, Dorn?"

Her voice was an uncanny impersonation of Maj. Kachem's, and Dorn could not help but smile. He laughed longer than was necessary. It helped lessen his tension, and he said in a conciliatory tone, "We are up against an unconventional force, which we engage with conventional means, instead of trying to reach the minds and souls of those whom we want to convert to our side. We are engaged in a battle we cannot win. We'd have a better chance of winning against communists, socialists, or terrorists, than fighting the Church—"

"We are not fighting the Church. We are fighting the Company—"

"Come now, Captain. Centuries of unrelenting efforts have reaped rewards. In parts of the world the Company is the only Church the faithful know and listen to. The Jesuits have the ears of the very grassroots whom we stand against. We hunt down their missionaries, we capture them, imprison, or kill. Yet we fail, time and again, to kill what they represent."

She looked at him, her eyes probing, drilling deep into the sockets, and beyond. She said nothing, but in her gaze he recognized concurrence.

He held his own, and pressed harder, "No point soaping each other's eyes. We both know we're going to do our best, but I think we agree our measures are short-sighted—"

He could have expected anything but the look she returned. Their eyes met and for a brief moment they were as close mentally as they were physically, their minds rubbing one against the other as their elbows.

"You folks won't mind my joining you?"

The voice startled both. It belonged to a man in his sixties, who was holding a tin of beer, and leaning over the vacant alley seat next to Dorn. The stranger did not wait for an invite and collapsed onto the seat with a gasp. His eyes were bloodshot and glazed, his face bloated. It was clear the man indulged in alcohol, the early morning beer likely part of daily routine.

"Helborn. Foras Helborn." He introduced himself with a belch, and added, "I couldn't help notice you at the airport, with Will Kachem."

Alarm bells rang in Dorn's head. Maj. Kachem's presence was overwhelming, if only by proxy. In his state of mind, expecting treachery every minute of every day, Dorn assumed the man was Kachem's eyes and ears. He looked closer into the small drunken eyes, set closely together, made the smaller by a forehead extended to a balding head. Despite the alcohol, the eyes retained their shrewdness. They were the eyes of someone who, despite the apparent intoxication, was able to command a clear mind.

"Who?" Dorn asked neutrally.

The impertinent man was a loud talker. Not making en effort to keep the conversation private, he cried, "Will Kachem, that's who!" Suddenly his expression turned to mock apologetic. "Pardon me. Don't think it my habit to bother perfect strangers, but your acquaintance with Will makes us— How does it go? Friends of my friends are—"

It was no point pretending anymore. In order to contain the loudmouthed man. Dorn asked, "You too work in the Building, then?"

"In, or for, who doesn't these troubled days?" If Helborn expected a reply he did not have the patience to stare into Dorn's inexpressive eyes. He changed the subject.

"You two heading for holidays?"

"We're not together," the woman said hurriedly.

"Aw, my apologies, my apologies. Mea culpa, as they say down there," Helborn pointed to the land below. He quickly added in a conspiratorial voice, "Not that your secret isn't safe with me. Those lips are sealed."

What play the man was putting on Dorn could not fathom. On the one hand the straight acknowledgment of acquaintance was consistent with tactics of intimidation used by Kachem, on the other the obnoxious appearance and approach could not hold to achieve the desired effect. Thus a pressing and unforeseen obstacle required attention — who was this man Helborn, and what were his intentions?

Evidently Capt. Weader's mind worked along the same lines when she asked, "What takes you south, Mr. Helborn?"

"That, which lures you there as well, I'm sure. The sun, the people, the lifestyle, la mañana, to which I'd like to raise the wrist." True to his word he finished with a loud swig.

"You're a sightseeing man?" Dorn asked.

"Me? I live for the architecture. Whew, it blows your mind down there. Those cathedrals that rival any in Europe. And what about all those mission churches the Jesuits built, eh?"

With his bloodshot eyes on Dorn, a minute grin contracting his lips, Helborn winked.

This was too much for Capt. Weader. Her face pale, she turned to the window.

Only two more hours of this brute, Dorn thought. He was wrong by a long shot...

The three-storey hotel on Plaza Catedral was a busy and popular place. Its claim to fame was an extended, if distant visit by a much celebrated writer. Despite its prime location the hotel was in a state of gradual demise. Its rooms were small and dim, and fresh paint could not hide cracked stucco, while sagging foundations made it impossible to open closed windows, as well as to close ones already open. It was just as well, Dorn opined, for the neglect drove the more demanding Gringos to more comfortable lodging across the square, thus reducing the possibility of meeting unforeseen acquaintance.

With the Capt. Weader already checked in and riding in an elevator up, Dorn made it a point to request a room directly above hers, and was filling the required information when he heard the familiar voice, followed by a pat on the shoulder.

"We're in one of those fortunate places where Euringos don't outnumber us Gringos. So, fancy us meeting again!"

Foras Helborn was smiling from ear to ear.

Dorn could not think of an answer. It was indeed a most unlikely coincidence to have met an acquaintance of Maj. Kachem's, made still more improbable by sharing the same hotel.

Helborn was not put off by the silent treatment.

"Where is your charming companion? She promised to have a cerveza with me, and she strikes me as the sort of woman to follow through on her promises."

It was true. Vague about their lodgings, they both offered vague promises of meeting again, only to rid themselves of the pesky man. Apparently they would not avoid his company after all.

"We're not companions," Dorn replied at last.

"Good, good!" Helborn ran his thick tongue over his lips.

Perplexed, suspecting Kachem's hand in Helborn's presence, Dorn said nothing. Why would the Major pick a man so obnoxious, someone whose ability to make himself repelling trampled any possible chances of succeeding in whatever his mission entailed? To befriend the target in order to conduct close observation was not an easy task, but to aggravate the subject offered no prospects for a successful mission, unless one aimed to elicit a particular response. Was Helborn trying to unnerve Dorn, or was his appearance on the scene a mere coincidence? Whether a snitch, or simply a drunkard with unrestrained mouth, he could cause trouble, Dorn thought. Something would have to be done about one Foras Helborn.

16. Fate Escapes No One

Casa Presidencial.
In the small chamber adjoining the President's office, and used chiefly for private audiences, and meetings kept off the record, sat two uniformed men, each occupying a comfortable chair. Surrounded by sumptuous decoration, they felt the power of the office pressing down on them. Despite the plush setting both faces expressed discomfort and the will to be anyplace but here. Their faces contorted the more at the appearance of yet another man, whose eyes did not match the festive mood suggested by his evening tuxedo.

The newcomer entered through a side door, and sat on the high leather seat belonging to the President, who was downstairs, entertaining the most illustrious families of the nation. To say the man was displeased was a huge understatement. He was fuming, but an old bird that he was, he dressed none of it in words. Rather, it was evident in the silence with which he greeted the uniformed men.

Expecting an explosion the two officers glanced at one another.

The gesture was not missed and roused the civilian.

"The circle is coming to a close, at last," he said with a bloodthirsty spark in his eyes.

They dared not speak. Despite holding the highest military ranks, in effect commanding the country's armed forces between them, they could not bring themselves to look into the civilian's eyes. In a country where a handful wielded almost absolute power, the military was only a tool, and its commanders obedient dogs ready to act as directed. They looked up to the man as dogs to their master. This was the man most powerful among the fourteen families without whose express wishes no law was passed, no government official was elected, no officer promoted, and no business deal approved.

"Explain how it came about," commanded the privileged one.

They exchanged quick glances before one of them replied.

"Our people, who work in the Building, intercepted a message in an old Nahuatl. We weren't able to decode it, but we traced the message to its recipient. He's the one."

Again time passed before the man replied, his voice quiet, the voice of a predator preparing to strike, "Bring him to me."

"It shall be done," said one of the officers.

"But what about the Gringos? They want him, too," the other added in a penitent voice.

The man looked down on the officers who held the two most senior positions in the military, but acted as schoolboys. He was not upset with them, though. He enjoyed the reaction his mere presence evoked. A little fear now and then kept the house in order.

"Chinga the Gringos!" he said. "I want him, and I should think, Gen. Putocara, that you'd like to lay your hands on him, too!"

The man addressed by the penguin had straightened his back. Sparks in his eyes said all there was to say...

It was shortly after 3 a.m. that November night, over twenty years ago. When the call came through the officer was not asleep. Rather, he was pacing nervously around the small bare room that belonged to the General Staff. It was located only several hundred meters away from the events he had orchestrated, but with the unrest and fighting going on throughout the city he could not isolate the gunshots he so wanted to hear. He heard the explosions and the machine gun fire through the open windows, but those could have come from other incidents, after all the civil war was in full swing, Still, he knew the plan was underway, he could depend on his people to carry out his orders unconditionally in those days when to kill was to live. At last, after an agonizing hour of waiting, the call came. He picked up the shortwave radio. The message was what he expected it to be, 'The swine are dead.' He breathed in with relief then, much as he did now. It was not until the morning of the next day that he learned the terrible truth that would haunt him for years to come: the body count did not add up. He examined the pictures taken by his henchmen. It was true: only six priests lay dead, where seven were expected. Worse still, later reports in the foreign media cited an eyewitness, a priest who observed the military storm the University building and chanting their slogan: *Be a patriot — Kill a Priest*. But a priest survived, and he saw the executions. A priest who saw the faces of the executioners. A priest who got away...

Now, more than twenty years later it still made the officer shudder with anger. Six priests lay dead. Six lay dead where seven ought to be. One escaped his fate, but fate escapes no one. And now the Seventh has returned to meet his fate. At last.

17. Blast from the Past

Showered, shaved, and dressed in a pair of light khakis he picked up in a store adjacent to the hotel, Dorn was ready to explore the surroundings in search of several indispensables. His main concern were the shoes, heavy, military stock, impossible in the humid climate. With that thought in mind he reached for the door handle and froze at the sound of a knock. He hesitated a minute. This could not be Hollie Weader, as they agreed on keeping their acquaintance a secret. It could not be Brother Anselm, either, since their meeting was scheduled elsewhere. Who, then?

The knock was persistent, vigorous, the sort of knowing knock delivered when the inhabitants were expected inside.

Dorn opened.

The huge man wore a uniform whose seams tested the limits of the threads used to sew the buttons. He pushed through the door, and walked in passed Dorn without a word. He stopped in the middle of the room, his back to the balcony door.

Dorn watched him without a word, something oddly familiar in the officer's countenance causing his consternation. He was convinced they had met before, his mind searching for an instant in time associated with terrifying memories. He focused on the winded face covered with creased lines, the square jaw, and predatory eyes, and remembered. His face paled...

Following the seminary, Kamil continued his education at the Jesuit Universidad, located only a short distance from the Plaza Catedral. He divided his time between lectures in the capital city, and attending to the wounded and sick at a provisional infirmary set up by the Jesuits in the Sierra Madre Mountains. Part of the teaching experience, his duties included everything from changing bedding and preparing meals, to administering medicines and cleaning the wounds. It was an exhaustive if fulfilling job, made the more rewarding through the study and understanding of the writings of the founder of the Order, to which he returned as opportunity awarded. The writings helped him find the necessary strength in the face of suffering of the people under his care. Those moments when he immersed himself in the study in solitude helped him retain the faith in the path chosen for him by the uncle, and reaffirmed by Brother Anselm. He would strap a knapsack filled with books and hike up the hill that overlooked the small luscious valley where the infirmary lay hidden. Only minutes away, it was a world away from the cries of pain, a perch on a rocky cliff, a magnificent vista of dark green jungle filled with the sounds of birds and a murmur of the creek below. It was an idyllic place removed from the troubles of the temporal world.

The idyll was short lived. It ended one sunny day, the day Kamil dozed off with the book in his hand. He woke up with his heart pounding. Heavy air hung around this pristine place, muffling all sounds — the chirping birds, the wind in the trees, and the murmur of the creek — as though the world had suddenly died. And then he heard it, the sound of death and dying, the unmistakable dry clicks of machine guns laced with cries of fear and pain.

The infirmary was under attack!

With the thick volume in his clenched fingers, the young man sprinted down the narrow and curving goat path with only one concern on his mind: His patients. He was nearing the last turn in the thicket of trees when he was stopped at his tracks by the sight of a contorted face, a face he would never forget. It belonged to a man wearing military slacks, a man whose entire concentration was on the volume in the young man's arms. Kamil's eyes wandered from the face, to the neck, and the arm, to the hand that held a shotgun. At the instant in time, between life and death, nothing else existed but the finger that squeezed the trigger.

When he came to, his heart was gripped with fear. His eyes were glued shut by blood from his forehead. He scraped off the crust. He felt the deep wound, he felt the onrush of fresh moist warmth, but he did not feel the pain, his mind in shock at what he saw in the sky. The sun was setting already, covered in dark grey ominous smoke. The smell of burned flesh dominated the air. He felt as though he was in a trance when he neared what once was the infirmary. He stood in horror as he observed the site. He felt life escaping through every pore of his skin, waning as the sun below the tree line.

Bullet-ridden, burned, tortured and decapitated corpses of patients, volunteers and staff, were spread out throughout, their thumbs tied behind their backs — a trademark of death squads. Hanged on the parched door frames were the terribly mutilated bodies of the Brothers, their eyes and tongues pulled out. The bodies of the female Sisters were spread on the ground, their faces slashed, hair burned, raped. Everyone was dead. Everyone was murdered in accordance with the death squads' motto — *Leave no witnesses...* Later, news reached him of the coordinated series of attacks in which thousands were slaughtered, bodies adding up so quickly the Junta could not bury them fast enough to cover the crime, of the stench of the decomposing flesh permeating vast areas of the western sections of the country.

Kamil could not cry. He could not shout. He could not pray. He did not feel. His mind was filled with the face of the man who held and aimed the shotgun, the same man who, years later, would face him in the hotel room.

"I'd like to hear that only the natural beauty of the land brought you here, Pvt. Dorn," the man started in good, if accented English, his voice guttural, rough.

Dorn could not speak. Afraid the expression on his face might betray him he took a step back, away from the sunlight. He dreaded facing the killer of his friends and patients, not because of fear, but because he was stricken with feelings he had not experienced since that tragic day in the Sierra Madres. He wanted to lunge at the man, to punch, to kick, and to punch more, until he would beat the life out of the murderer's face. He did not. Instead he stood still, struggling to regain control of himself.

Noticing the peculiar reaction, and reading it as a sign of weakness, the uniformed man continued, "Listen to me, amigo. Your presence here makes a lot of people very concerned. You can tell your bosses Chief Jorge del Toro will not let you fight your wars here. *Comprendo?*"

Dorn burst out laughing. The tension arisen from his own painful memories, combined with realization the killer did not recognize him, had caused the strange and unexpected reaction. The murderer of innocents, of ill and defenseless, the one who aimed and fired at the young student, did not recognize his victim. He would not, of course, for in mass murderer's eyes all faces fade out, as though the brain activates a mechanism to preserve the killer's sanity. Something else helped trigger Dorn's reaction. Chief del Toro knew things he should not. He knew Dorn's military employment, his rank and name. It meant a mole working with Karin Platt was only a small tribe in a big wheel of problems that would occupy Maj. Kachem. The

Building was a nest of spies, making it this much easier to blend in and disappear.

18. Sister Clare

Chief Jorge del Toro's memory might not have served him, but his visit rekindled Dorn's fear, this most prevailing fear, which haunted every spy, a fugitive, even an actor — the fear of betraying one's true identity despite every effort made to mask it. Dorn lived with this fear every day, it lingered in his mind, and was in the back of every thought. The most difficult task was conquering it, going about his daily duties despite the pervasive, sneaky thought of his eyes being the proverbial mirror into the soul. An absurd thought, perhaps, but it shaped his life, was responsible for the routine that helped keep the fear in check, and remain in control of his mind. A combination of exercises involving physical activity and meditation were instrumental in achieving the goal.

And so he rushed out of the hotel to tire, to suppress, and force the thoughts into retreat.

He meandered the streets of the city he had not seen in years. He did not know how long he had been out, or where his legs took him. Various sites passed by his unseeing eyes, from the Iglesia de la Compaña, to the busy Mercado. The latter, with its busy and rumpus crowds, succeeded at last in diverting his mind from the troubled visit. He strolled along its alleys and stalls until, gradually, the white noise of human chatter turned into discernible voices. Some of them were directed at him. It took some time to understand their meaning, some more to reply, if only by shaking his head in response to various products offered. The buzz, the constant flow of human bodies, the invigorating scent of ripe fruit, it all contributed to turning his attention away from the deadly memories.

He emerged from the covered market onto the street with his head partially clear. He had found the commanding officer of the death squad responsible for the murder of all the patients of the infirmary, himself having not suffered unmasking. He had waited for this moment for years, never expecting it to come to fruition, and he struggled now to set his burning desire to punish aside. He had to conquer it. He had to. He vowed he would make the man pay for his crimes, but he could not risk jeopardizing his mission.

Worried the anger could return and cloud his mind beyond his ability to control it, Dorn started briskly toward the plaza when he noticed a familiar figure brush against the shaded façades of the buildings that lined the opposite side of the street. Capt. Weader's face showed for a brief moment in the sun's reflections cast by windshields of oncoming vehicles. Was she following him? Everything about the way she rushed, as someone with a purpose, suggested her presence here coinciding with Dorn was only a twist of fate.

Dorn instinctively withdrew into the shades of the buildings, and followed the woman, keeping a distance of a half a block, using vehicles parked along the curb as additional cover.

Several blocks later the woman stopped abruptly, turning around as though she changed her mind. Old trick, Dorn thought. Anticipating the move for some time he was ready, and swiftly backed into a deep door recess. Noises behind his back drew his attention. He pressed his ear into the crack between the thick double doors, and peeked through it. He saw several young children, perhaps five years of age, holding a pup, pulling its paws, swinging it, flinging, the exhausted animal enduring it in numb, eerie silence.

Fascinated by the cruel game at the hands of the young Dorn lost the sight of Capt. Weader. By the time he stepped out of the dark shadow the woman was gone.

The residential area was home to a narrow group of middle class residents who had managed to hold on to their status despite growing poverty across the board. Houses here belonged to families with established roots in government and financial services. While not wealthy, they enjoyed the comfort of a slow depreciation of affluence compared to the shock therapy suffered by employees of manufacturing industries, even in this land of sweatshops unable to compete with cheap Asian imports. Houses here, although large, were often inhabited by four or five generations of family members living under the same roof. Some of the homes span half a city block, with huge gates providing privacy and serving as deterrents for prying eyes.

Searching for the woman behind those walls was no use. Dorn spent the next half hour of the waning daylight loitering in front of a nearby church, angry with himself for having failed so amateurishly. He would have waited longer, determined to find out what brought Capt. Weader to this part of town, and in such a conspiratorial way, had he not been late for a meeting of his own. Reluctantly he turned toward the central part of the old town.

Meanwhile…

"I'm looking for Tía Confianza," Maj. Hollie Weader said in fluent Spanish to the middle-aged woman who opened the door.

She followed inside, to a spacious courtyard encased by bright, if pale walls, each painted in a different pastel color. In one of the corners stood a large wooden weaving loom with half-finished replica of a well-known paining, woven using natural fibers in rich colors derived from native plants. Several throw rugs sporting folk patterns were scattered around the courtyard, a skein of yarn in the woman's hand suggesting she was the artist responsible for the creations. Numerous framed photographs and cutouts from color magazines and yellowed newspapers praised the accomplishments and sported awards received by one of the foremost weaving artists.

"I am Confianza," said the woman and placed the yarn on the elongated wooden table.

Still tense after trying to elude Dorn, Capt. Weader exhaled deeply and gave the first part of the prearranged password, "I want to commission a woven carpet suitable for a floor of a waiting room in my office."

The woman's pupils contracted momentarily but no muscle flexed on her face.

"I create only one-of-a-kind works of art," was her reply.

"I am sister Clare," said Capt. Weader. She reached underneath her blouse and drew out a silver cross she wore attached to a long silver chain. She approached, pulled the cross over her head and handed it to the woman. "I must see Father Giordano."

The woman looked her from toes to ears before she accepted the cross. She then walked over to a large wooden cabinet set against the orange wall. She found a pair of reading glasses and a magnifier, and thus armed she approached a standing lamp. She examined the cross closely, focusing on its intricate encrustations.

Apparently satisfied she projected a smile and, handing back the cross, she said, "We've been expecting you, Sister. Father Giordano has arrived last night."

"I must see him immediately," Capt. Weader said excitedly, and slipped the cross over onto her slender neck.

"I'm afraid it must wait."

"But—"

"No buts, Sister. Enhanced security measures are in place, and will be followed."

"But I must—" Weader protested.

"You will, Sister, in due course, when the security measures have been dutifully followed."

Tía Confianza went back to the cabinet, and picked up a small digital camera. She returned to her guest, and said, "Smile." She snapped a picture and reviewed it. Satisfied, she said, "Best if you not come back here again. We will contact you with further instructions."

"When?" Capt. Weader asked eagerly.

The woman glanced at the photograph once more before replying.

"These are trying times, Sister. Not everyone is who they say they are. Not everything is what it seems. The Company must be protected, and security procedures followed with extraordinary care. We shall contact you when the time comes."

19. Cataclysmic Awakening

The small plazuela was lined with sparsely grown palm trees. Dorn cut across its cobblestone center, past a dry water fountain, and approached a cast iron park bench surrounded by dense bougainvilleas. Occupying one end of the bench was a colorful man, a thick stash of folded newspapers resting beside him. His face, covered by the wide rim of a sombrero, was drooped to his chest. The wide hat, the colorful shirt with a high collar, and the darkness could not conceal the pale face, so unbecoming of a local. High leather boots, and a big shiny belt buckle, with sparkling reflections cast by lights of a shop across the street, completed the picture.

"I was worried something happened to you," the man said in Spanish.

Dorn looked closer. It was the same voice but the face... In the poor light the face did not match the voice.

"You're late, Kamil." The man smiled.

"Brother Anselm!" Dorn exhaled. "The moustache, the clothes... Is it tan? I did not recognize you. Your transformation is truly formidable!"

"Call me Anselmo," the man replied in English with an exaggerated Spanish accent.

Dorn did not laugh.

"Something the matter?" the elder asked.

Dorn sat down on the bench with a heavy thump. He described the visit from Chief del Toro, followed by his recollection of the events of the time of the civil war.

Brother Anselm's eyebrows creased.

"Everything happens for a reason. Do you remember the day our supply team found you at the site of the smoldering infirmary?"

Dorn looked into his friend's face. How could he forget.

"You were meant to experience this horrible event, just as our old Father General, God bless his soul, had experienced his cataclysmic event — to strengthen your resolve to serve those who need you the most. Remember what I told you then?"

Dorn remembered. Following the horror witnessed at the infirmary, he was devastated and dispirited. Brother Anselm sat with him, and told him about a cataclysmic event which had happened over half a century earlier, in a different part of the world, and which was responsible for the transformation of a man who would become the Father General of the Company, and would lead the Jesuits on a new path...

The view from the orchards on the slopes of the mountain spanned a magnificent vista of a sun-drenched valley stretching from sea to sea. The air had the sweet taste of cherry fruit hollowed by millions of bees and dried in the hot sun. Bird chirping resonated in a deafening cacophony of ear-pleasing tones. Below, in the outskirts of town, the peasants tended to their miniscule vegetable gardens, their melancholy songs reaching the higher ground on the gusts of gentle breeze. To the residents of the novitiate located up on the hill it seemed another day filled with study and prayer, the idyll occasionally broken by pesky, but seldom realized air-raid alarms. The alarms had ceased their piercing whine at seven that morning, quickly filling the young hearts with a promise of a tranquil day ahead. The war was raging, true, but it seemed so far away. A minute spent on reflections in the colorful paradise was an innocent moment to steal from an otherwise grief-stricken instant in time.

The peaceful moment changed suddenly, in the heartbeat that seemed to freeze in horror, in the blink of an eye that was a natural reaction to a source of light thousand times stronger than the Sun. It was the morning of August 6, 1945. The city stretched below was Hiroshima. The blinding light in the sky was the exploding "Little Boy", that mastery of the evil ingenuity of man. A shockwave that followed the blinding light turned all glass into myriads of little shards that penetrated the skin and eyes; the shockwave was chased by a high wind, which carried intense heat, flaked the skin of the living, and turned their bodies into screaming fireballs.

Within the hour the roads and paths leading from the charred city to the hills and the novitiate were filled with masses of scarred, burned, bleeding, injured and terrified survivors of the first nuclear attack conducted by and against human life. To all the Fathers, Brothers, and novices, who witnessed the carnage, it would forever serve as an example of the actions of a society that rejected God. The experience would turn their lives into a passionate crusade for teaching the love of God, but none would make as profound an impact on the lives of millions as did the young Basque Father who would later lead the most powerful Catholic Order on the path of change.

The young Father offered first-aid help to the scores of injured as they ascended the novitiate in search of temporal assistance and the spiritual empowerment in their last moments before taking the leap into the great after, the promised Heaven. They would receive both, for the Basque

Father was not only a doctor of the soul, he was a healer of the mortal coil, too. Having studied medicine in Europe, he operated on the injured on his desk with what little equipment was on hand. He and his fellow Brothers tended to the needy until their medical supplies run out. They cleaned the wounds of the sick, and healed the souls of those who had the capacity to embrace forgiveness. They remained at their posts, prowling the burning city streets for weeks, bringing help to the needy, Unction to the dying — both received with gratitude, for in light of the tragedy it did not matter what religion represented the priest who performed the last rites that began the journey to God.

The experience of Hiroshima fueled the Father's relentless drive for change: to bring God where God was previously cast off. The cataclysmic event convinced him that only a Godless society could permit itself to commit acts of such atrocity. It convinced him that an equally devastating destiny awaited the millions who suffered oppression and injustice around the world. He never lost the conviction that an antidote to violence, hunger and misery existed in the pedagogy of love; that a world was within reach, a world in which man did not exist to annihilate another, but a world where man lived in commitment to social Gospel of love for human brethren. And it was this conviction and the resulting philosophy, which helped him become elected to lead the most power Catholic Order on the path to change, to a New, a Better World.

20. Dark Thoughts

"I grieve with you, my son," Brother Anselm said. "Finding the beast who torched the infirmary is indeed a terrifying discovery. It must, and will be addressed, but not when it could jeopardize your current mission." He raised his arm to silence Dorn's opposition, and added, "Everything in due course. You must leave it aside for now, and concentrate on the issue at hand." And as though to make his decision final he asked in a forceful voice, which accepted no objection, "Tell me everything that was said during the visit. Omit nothing."

Silence followed as Dorn struggled with his emotions. It took time before he could gather words to describe the Chief's brief visit in detail, albeit in a trembling voice.

Brother Anselm said when the account was over, "They know who you are, and it is for the better for they won't dare touch you."

"Perhaps you're right, but there is something troubling in his insistence to stay out of the country's internal affairs. It suggests an action against the Company."

"As bad as it sounds we can use this foreknowledge to prepare ourselves against their strike."

"Theirs? Who are they?"

"I think we both know the answer, no?"

Indeed, he did, for in this country nothing was done without the knowledge and approval of the fourteen families, which dominated all affairs of the small state.

A brightly dressed woman with an armful of colorful shawls approached the bench. Ignoring the sombreroed man she presented her products to the young Gringo. She was not discouraged by his lack of interest and continued to display a greater variety of goods she held in a cloth sack, which she carried on her shoulder. Dorn purchased something to send the woman on her way, but the move only brought several more vendors from the shadows, each eager to make a sale. Their persistence went on, and would have continued if not for Brother Anselm, whose unbecoming firmness put an end to the siege.

The intermission, though short, calmed Dorn's nerves.

With the streetsellers at a safe distance to carry on the conversation, Brother Anselm changed the subject, "Our friends did some research on Capt. Weader."

"She's notoriously famous in intelligence circles," Dorn said.

"Indeed, her successes are very troubling for us."

"What boggles the mind is her ability to penetrate our networks."

"Not so surprising if you consider she operates under the cryptonym of Sister Clare, of the Dominican Sisters. The identity opens many a door."

"Can we stop her?"

Brother Anselm shook his head.

"Sister Clare, vel Capt. Weader, works with SITGRA—"

"What the Devil is that?"

"Special Intelligence Task Group for Religious Affairs. It's a joint affair between the Dottrina and your military intelligence."

"You mean the Holy See sanctions her work against the clergy?"

"The exact specifics of SITGRA's are kept secret from us, it's existence is not even acknowledged, but you can fill the blanks."

"But she receives help from somewhere, if only to provide her with an identity!"

"Bah, this is the easiest part. Mention you are on a quest to destroy the Company and the willing shall line up. Have you heard the latest anecdote about the Dominicans? The *domini canes*, the hounds of God, offer absolution to anyone who reports on liberalizing Jesuits. You see, my boy, we gain followers, which scares the bejesus out of the Hierarchy, but with each soul we save we attract another, dead set on destroying us. These spread awful lies about us, they make up conspiracies involving the Company, and which outnumber even those attributed to Jews. The bewitching machinery has done plenty over the centuries to discredit our work. We can't seem to shake the stigma of being the architects of the drive for a new world order—"

"But we are!" Dorn objected excitedly.

"We want a better world, and the grassroots know it, but the general ignorant laic society knows only what it hears on corporate media. Ask anyone what they think of the Company, and they will quote any number of conspiracies overheard on television. A television set, present in every household, had become one of the biggest obstacles to positive progress in the world. Why? Because it keeps the people brainwashed, and locked inside, under self-imposed house arrest, when, instead, they should go out, onto the streets."

"This is where we come in! Our missionaries work on the streets, with the grassroots, to change the world. Their work is reaping rewards, and my presence here as agent of the most powerful military in the world is proof of it. The Superpower is afraid—"

Dorn fell silent at a gentle nudge on the ribs. Three young policemen appeared out of the shadows, shooting more than customary glances as they passed by the bench.

"We better wrap it up," Brother Anselm did not like the look on the policemen's faces.

"Who is Weader receiving support from?"

"The Opus Dei, undoubtedly."

"Can you put a tail on her?"

"Is it absolutely necessary? Our Invisible Company resources are stretched beyond limits, what with the civil war sparks flying around the country."

"It is imperative to reach the courier before the woman does."

"You think she may reach him before you do?"

"It is something we must avoid at all cost."

"Trailing her may expose our agents."

"They know the risks they take."

"Do you realize what they risk? Members of the Invisible Company are not ordained priests. They are lay people who are committed to supporting the Order. As such they cannot count on blanket cover enjoyed by the clergy. The Opus Dei spies are only too happy to expose them to the secret police. We cannot endanger them. We cannot afford to jeopardize their network, not at a time when we may need to rely on them as never before. The country is on the brink of another civil war, and when it escalates the priests will be detained, deported, or disappeared, as they were the last time. No, Kamil, we can not ask our agents to sidetrack from their main objective to prepare base in case of war. Besides, I don't think I can reach them in time, for they are underground, so deep it would take days, time we do not have. You and I are the only resource we can count on at the moment. And I think we stand as good a chance as Capt. Weader in reaching the courier, perhaps even better for we know of the woman's true objectives."

"Between the two of us we cannot follow her every move."

Brother Anselm thought for a minute before replying, "Perhaps, then, we ought to orchestrate such conditions, which would prompt miss Weader to seek our company, to keep her close?"

Dorn considered the thought.

"By our company, you mean mine."

Brother Anselm said nothing.

"My failure and exposure would endanger the courier," Dorn said cautiously.

"If push comes to shove Capt. Weader's mission will be terminated. You have my word."

Dorn thought about the effects of experiences of a life on the margins of human existence. Here was a man whose entire life was dedicated to pious and unswerving perseverance in the cause of good — a jovial and deeply spiritual man who, in a roundabout way, has suggested the worst sin of all. His eyes penetrating through the darkness and shadows, Dorn tried to look into his friend's eyes. Perhaps he read more in the words than Brother Anselm meant? Resolving to the ways of the enemy, even for such cause as to protect the network upon which so many lives depended, went against everything he learned at the seminary, against everything the Company stood for. Was it against Dorn's own convictions? A completed seminary was not priesthood. Nonetheless, did his service for the Company not come with certain moral and ethical obligations? How was he to read Brother Anselm's words?

Brother Anselm broke his musings. He tapped on the newspaper, which rested beside him on the bench.

"Inside is something you may find helpful to carry out the assignment."

Dorn swallowed hard. Expecting to find a firearm his fingers fumbled between the folded pages. Something fell on the ground. He reached down and found a small object.

"A key?" Dorn was perplexed.

"You may need to move fast around the city. A moped is parked at the lot behind the cathedral…"

21. First Contact

Dorn strolled back to Plaza Catedral. Despite, or perhaps because of the troubles brewing in the country, with tremors of civil war shaking the minds and hearts, Saturday evening crowds descended upon the plaza in droves. Expecting eruption of violence any day, the people lived day-to-day, embracing the opportunity to enjoy a peaceful evening, perhaps the last one in a long time. Certainly nothing suggested the onset of the bloody strife, and the plaza was turned into the venue it served every weekend, and most evenings. Fold out chairs set around the central pagoda were occupied by folk eager to play, to enjoy life, to forget about the dark clouds, which covered the sky over their country. Here and there children played with enormous tube balloons, throwing them into the sky, chasing.

Dorn made a customary round about the plaza, and ended up outside a busy restaurant nested under the arches, where a street musician played a guitar, entertaining the patrons. Waiters moved lethargically with trays of alcohols on their shoulders. None resembled the man whose face Dorn committed to memory. Time passed, and he was beginning to worry whether he found the correct locale, when the familiar face emerged from the inside of the restaurant. It took still more time before a table became available in the section the waiter was responsible for. At last Dorn took a seat facing the plaza and the guitar player. A steady flow of couples, and singles, passed by, but the waiter did not approach. Dorn turned around and remained in the position until he made eye contact with the man he sought. He was a slightly hunched, ghastly figure with thin greasy hair he wore quaffed all the way back, his crooked grin missing several teeth. He dusted the burgundy tablecloth with his serviette and handed Dorn the menu without a word.

"*Buenas noches, señor* Fink," Dorn opened in Spanish. He continued in English, "Regards from the headquarters for your loyal service."

If Chad Fink was surprised his facial expression did not show it. Instead he seemed to grow taller as his hunched back straightened momentarily. His eyes shifting side to side, he opened the menu and leaned over the customer as though describing the available dishes.

"Pvt. Dorn. I hear you were paid a visit from Chief del Toro."

Dorn ground his teeth. So much for the assumed identity provided by Maj. Kachem. Everyone seemed to know who he was.

Not seeing a point in denying his identity, Dorn replied, "News spreads fast in this town."

"Only if one knows how to listen."

"I gather that you know how and where. Can we talk privately?" Dorn shot a telling look to a neighboring table where a family consumed their meal in silence.

"Not here. I'm working the night shift. Meet me tomorrow at the same time by the fountain at the Arena Park. Know where it is?"

"I'll find it." Dorn nodded and wanted to ask another question, but Fink walked off and disappeared inside the restaurant.

He returned several minutes later with a large mug of freshly brewed chocolate.

"Local specialty, *señor*," he announced aloud.

"It is urgent that we speak tonight, Fink," Dorn pressed in a lower voice.

"No rush. It's the South, the land of *mañana*. In any case, you can't reach the man you came to see before Monday."

"Has he not arrived yet?" Dorn asked with hope.

"Oh, he's here, alright," Fink said with a sarcastic grin, his eyes looking down on Dorn. He added icily, "But so is the traitor, and additional security measures are observed. Now, act like you're enjoying your choco, and leave some change when you're done. They don't pay me enough for what I'm worth, you know."

Dorn did not touch the tempting drink. One did not accept strong beverages, which could be used to conceal the color, taste, and scent of an unknown substance. It was part of playing the shadow game, always on guard; wearying at first it became second nature. He had no concrete reasons to mistrust Fink, despite the snitch's ominous statement. How could Fink know the identity of the mole? Yet, uncertainty burrowed in his mind, and Dorn could not help but wonder about the greasy man's sources. It was a pointless exercise, one which produced more doubt. He needed to divert his mind.

He left some coins on the table, and joined a flow of men and women on a stroll around the plaza. Passing restaurants with live music and cheerful chatter of the patrons helped rid his mind of the unpleasant visions. They were soon replaced with the slim, tanned figure of the woman. He summoned the vivid images of the thin skirt that embraced the wide hips, and the shirt that accentuated the slim waist. He recalled the lagoon eyes. Inadvertently his right hand touched his left elbow, the very part, which some hours prior, brushed against the woman's skin. He felt blood rush in his veins. He no longer thought of the woman as Capt. Weader, but simply as Hollie. As he explored the visions of the dazzling woman further he soon found himself in dangerous territory. Hollie Weader was not only a beautiful woman he could easily fall for. She was the enemy first and foremost.

22. Chance for Salvation

Someone was in his room. Dorn felt the presence the moment he pressed the door handle. It was too late to turn away, and he opened the door.

Capt. Hollie Weader was sitting in the easy chair, a bottle and two shot glasses on the table next to her. The balcony door was open, tunes of live music from the square poured inside.

"You followed me today. Why?" she opened without much ado.

He turned around to lock the doors, but more importantly to buy himself time.

"I was worried about you," he said at last.

Her voice devoid of gratitude, she said, "Thank you, but it wasn't necessary."

"The country is on the brink of a civil war. Confusion everywhere. The stakes are extremely high, and our opponents might seize the opportunity to strike."

She studied his face in the flicks of light falling from lampposts on the plaza.

"No need to demonize the adversary."

He was taken aback by her statement. Not certain how to read it, he said, "The Company has been accused of many heresies and devious conspiracies."

"Between you and me we can forget this Opus Dei propaganda," she replied sparingly.

Capt. Weader was full of surprises that night. He looked at her with curiosity.

"We must take up a position in order to fight them," he said. "The better we know them, the less blood may be spilled."

She reached to the bottle and filled the two shot glasses. With a sweeping gesture she invited him to take the other seat.

"Come now, Dorn. We're not dealing with thugs. The only blood spilled would be of the Jesuits dying martyr's deaths."

He sat down, and only now, from up close, did he notice the bottle was already half empty.

"Do not forget the priests who fight alongside the guerillas in many parts of the continent," he said to rouse her intoxicated mind.

She hung a long gaze on him before replying.

"You come prepared. I like that." She took a swig and continued, "The Company has changed in these past decades. Today's Jesuits carry AK-47s along with their crosses—"

"Weapons?" he cut in with doubting intonation that was aimed to encourage the woman to explicate.

"They fought and continue to fight along the revolutionaries in Africa, here, and all across the Americas, from Nicaragua and Guatemala, to Chile and Peru. Some turn to politics, and become advisers to presidents and labor unions, whereas others pick up shovels and build low-cost housing or sanitary sewage systems in rural areas…

Desperate situations call for desperate measures." She refilled and raised her glass, and waited for Dorn to click his.

The woman was well informed. Alarm bells rang in Dorn's head, and he could not help but wonder: Why was she really here? He wanted to look into her eyes, but to no avail. Capt. Weader was only a silhouette against the aureole of light pouring in from the plaza. He could detect change in her, but could not decide whether it was the alcohol, or something else, which had happened during her evening stroll. It altered his own perception of the woman. Underneath the outside persona of the notorious spy hunter he saw a human soul. A soul lost in the vast sea of evil. He welcomed the opportunity to save her.

"If it wasn't for the half empty bottle of Mezcal, I'd say you were converted," he said with a wink, his eyes piercing the dim space between them.

He could feel her eyes on him. It was not until this moment when he realized he had not switched on the lights. She did not ask him to turn them on, and it told him that both had secrets they did not want revealed.

"Being respectful of one's opponent is only wise," she said at last.

"But expounding on their virtues shows weakness in one's own convictions."

"You don't trust me," she said after a pause. "This why you followed me?"

Baffled by the question he took a swig and quickly extended his hand for a refill. His mind was racing. The mysterious and feared Capt. Weader was sitting in his room, drinking alone. What he would not give to understand the reasons behind the woman's insecurity!

"Maj. Kachem trains us to be vigilant at all times."

He knew he hit a sore spot when the woman replied through her teeth.

"Kachem may be a good theoretician, but his tactics do not serve him well as of late."

"He did catch Karin Platt."

She waved her arm dismissively.

"His tactic is similar to trawling the sea bottom for shrimp, catching everything that moves, and causing more damage than good. Platt was only the go between, and her capture alerted others, bigger fish."

"Others?"

"She could not have been acting alone. And even so, in the unlikely event that she was, there would be others. The Building is a bull's mark target for all agencies of the world. It is a given that more spies operate inside. It's a question of rooting them out."

"I take it your tactics are different?"

"You take it right."

She downed her glass, and set it on the table.

"But enough of that," she said in a changed voice. "Have you talked to Fink?"

"Says the courier is already here, and he'll tell more next time we meet."

"When?"

"Same time tomorrow."

"Where?"

He told her. Then he added, "There's more. Fink said the mole is here, too."

He thought the statement would in turn prompt her to reveal whatever she knew, but the woman did not lead on. She sat still for a time.

"It doesn't take a genius to figure it out," she said at last. "If the courier is here to pick up the package, then someone must deliver it."

"Have you found out who?" He took care not to let his voice betray his anxiety.

"All in due course," she said.

"But we must get to him before he reaches the courier."

"Do not be hasty. Kachem did enough damage already. Better tell me something about yourself. Help the time pass."

"I saw my service file in your folder," his voice could not conceal anger with the woman's elusiveness.

She filled the glasses, again.

"I don't mean that. I know what uniform you wear. But I don't know who you are. What makes you?"

"I could ask the same of you."

She raised her glass, and downed it.

"I was right. You don't trust me. Kachem put you up to it, didn't he? That envious es-o-be!" She turned the glass in her fingers, and said, "Alright. I was an army brat. My father worked his way up the ladder through bases in more countries than most of our compatriots could name. When he became a military attaché we moved from the barracks into much nicer embassy compounds. But not that much nicer. The world was changing, government after government was turning red, and our embassies became fortresses. It was then I first heard about Liberation Theology."

Dorn reached for his glass. It was empty. He refilled it, and could not help his hand tremble ever so slightly.

She watched him with intensity.

"Liberation Theology?" he repeated after her, the glass at his lips.

"I knew it was serious by watching my father go up in arms. Single biggest threat to our interests, he used to say. And the Company was at the forefront of it. They were making huge gains. Their strategy was simple and brilliant — global conversion through an enormous spiritual and sociological experiment across all classes, from peasants to elites. The Jesuits were the ideal missionaries for the movement that shook the world. From work in the smallest communities in the Third World, to elite private schools owned and operated by the Order, they turned the world upside-down. Against their work there were no weapons, yet we continued to shoot, and bomb. It got us nowhere. We were losing the hearts and minds of the people we wanted to turn to our side."

"This why you became a spy? To infiltrate the Company and its Liberation Theology supporters? To destroy them from within?"

"I have changed nothing."

"Your successes are the subjects of tales."

"Define success."

Something in her voice struck Dorn. Were Capt. Weader's sins so grave that she needed someone who would listen to her, to cleanse her conscience?

"You're making a difference," he egged.

She put down her glass, but did not reach for a refill.

"It's a beautiful world out there, Dorn. The people are beautiful, but the ideologues bring out the worst in us. Look at you. You're young, but your mind is already poisoned. You're pursuing ghosts when you should be courting some nice girl. Politics with its parties and ideologies, religions, languages and borders, it all exists only to pitch us one against another. Success, you say? There are no winners when we fight. We all lose."

Dorn did not reply immediately. Was the woman's tear-jerker testimony supposed to elicit a like one in response? If so, her attempt seemed crude, but the alcohol, the dimmed lights, and the gentle sounds from the plaza, aided the woman in creating an ambiance suitable for a confession. Someone less experienced would have perhaps fallen for the beautiful woman's trickery.

Suddenly she stood up, and extended her hand.

"Come, Dorn. Let us forget about the things, which separate us. Let us forget about what brought us here. Let tonight be about the things that make us beautiful."

She led him to the door, and down the creaky staircase to the plaza. They strolled toward the pagoda, led to it on the waves of string music. They mingled with couples of all ages. They danced, and danced, and nothing else mattered that night.

23. Inside Joke

Dorn woke up with a headache. His mind immediately and inadvertently turned to the woman. He took a cold shower to cure the headache and the persistent image. Somewhat refreshed he opened the curtains, and cursed aloud. The sun was high. He glanced at his wristwatch. He cursed. So much for the plan to follow Hollie, but to follow he was determined.

He dressed quickly and rushed out. Passing by the reception desk he noticed the key to the woman's room. He cursed under his breath. It was no use to run around the city looking for her. He decided to breakfast at a nearby restaurant with a patio offering a good scouting point. He chose a small table underneath a potted tropical plant, and awaited his order while chatting the co-occupant of the table — a large colorful parrot named Pepe who rocked back and forth on the armrest of the opposite chair.

Dorn breakfasted for a good hour, but Hollie Weader did not show up. Still the leisurely time was not altogether disagreeable. The sun warmed his bones, the swinging bird calmed his mind, and the happy faces of passersby helped divert his mind from the problems, which loomed ahead. Immersing himself in the slow pace of the Sunday morning he thought about Brother Anselm. It reminded him of the key he received from his friend. Perhaps the moped would come in handy in more ways than to aid in fulfilling his mission? He thought about the hills outside the city, and decided to find the time for them.

He glanced at the clock tower, and sighed. It was time. He paid the bill, and crossed the street, but after several steps he was struck with the peculiar sensation known to all fugitives and conspirators. His gut feeling told him that someone was following him. He changed direction, and employed the basic tactics taught by the escape and evasion course, but to no avail — he could not make out his pursuer, and blamed the suspicion on his heightened anxiety

Sunday filled the Company church with worshippers, and Dorn elbowed his way through crowds until he found the familiar figure seated at an agreed upon bench, a large sombrero resting beside, saving the seat for Dorn. He arrived none too late. The priest entered the altar, and the worshipper stood up.

"In the name of the Father, the Son, and the Holy Spirit," the priest opened.

"Amen," the congregation replied.

"The Lord be with you."

"And with your Spirit."

The mass had started, the priest's voice poured from the speakers, and Dorn turned to his neighbor. Just as he lowered his head to speak closely to the ear of the elderly man he froze. He felt sharp pricks in his neck, and turned his head abruptly to face the source of the prickly sensation. A pair of intensely blue eyes stared back at him. Those were the eyes of the woman he danced with into the wee hours of the morning. They expressed disillusionment mixed with triumph, before disappearing into the thick crowd.

"This time Capt. Weader has followed me," Dorn whispered to his companion.

Brother Anselm replied in like manner, without turning his head, "A worthy adversary for you, she is."

"Let's hope she's merely trawling the sea bottom."

Brother Anselm shot him a non-comprehending glance.

"An inside joke," Dorn clarified.

"Since when do you share inside jokes?"

Dorn lowered his head so as not to make eye contact with the neighbors who were casting curious glances, but more importantly he wanted to avoid the smart and penetrating eyes of his companion.

"It merely implies that she is only fishing."

They were speaking only when the priest recited the rites, and the congregation replied. It ensured privacy in the thick of the crowd, but made the conversation cumbersome.

"Have you given her reason to follow you?" Brother Anselm asked at the earliest opportunity to do so.

"Cannot imagine why she would."

"Perhaps it is not professional curiosity alone that brought her here?"

Their eyes locked. Dorn blushed. He and Hollie danced, talked, and laughed together. They spent a romantic evening together, but how much of it was dictated by a need to get to know the other on a professional level, and how much was in response to a heart's desire? To think that Hollie was interested in him for reasons other than purely professional was flattering, but he could not take it at face value. It disagreed with everything he had learned about the woman who was one of the most ruthless mole hunters. Simultaneously another thought shot through his head: Was she not a human being, too? Did she not display her human face? He recalled the conversion, her body language, and the timbre of her voice. Her performance seemed genuine. But what if it was only a performance? And what if she thought the same of him? Parts of the evening were blurry to Dorn.

Was it possible that his performance, however well rehearsed, had raised the woman's doubts?

Dorn glanced at his companion. Brother Anselm appeared engrossed in the mass. His lips moved in sync with the priest's, and his eyes expressed wonder at the irrevocability of the Church as represented by the mass — the same, word for word, in every part of the world. As Dorn observed his friend he was struck with sudden realization. The look in Hollie's eyes suddenly became clear to him. If he had any doubts earlier it was time to put them aside. Capt. Weader had connected the man from the sketch with the one sitting next to Dorn.

The ministrants prepared for the Eucharist, and the faithful began to rise from their seats. The commotion permitted a freer conversation.

"Do you think she recognized me?" Brother Anselm read in Dorn's mind.

It would take an uncommonly observant eye to make the connection between the rancher sitting next to him, and the face from the drawing, but Dorn could not delude himself any longer.

"Yes," he replied. "It highlights the need for a quick resolution."

Brother Anselm shook his head.

"We cannot speed up what we do not control."

"We must—" Dorn started forcefully.

"Shh—" Brother Anselm looked around, and continued in a low voice, "We cannot rely on the local network. The Fathers are under surveillance, and the Invisible Company is stretched to the limits, preparing for the worst."

Dorn persisted, "I shall meet Fink tonight. He insinuated he can make out the courier and the mole. We cannot sit idly by!"

"Snitches always do that," Brother Anselm shrugged dismissively. "They say what you want to hear. It's how they make themselves appear indispensable."

The thought was not improbable and Dorn relaxed somewhat.

The mass ended and they left the church with the flow of a large crowd. They spent time making certain they were not followed, and Brother Anselm led the way to a residential area where he introduced Dorn to a beat-up model of a popular Japanese sedan. He sat behind the wheel and invited Dorn to the passenger seat with a pillow stuffed in the cavity where a seat ought to be. Old newspapers, soda bottles, and many unidentified items cluttered the floor and the back seat.

"You really know how to treat yourself," Dorn said. He picked up a moldy sandwich from the dashboard and threw it to a skinny dog who followed them from the church. The animal swallowed the sandwich with hardly any chewing, its eyes asking for more. Dorn turned his eyes, unable to face the misery of the innocent creature.

Brother Anselm started the engine.

"You can leave it unlocked and no one will touch it. Besides, looks can be deceiving."

He revved the engine, scaring the animal, and demonstrated the ease with which the vehicle took off. He drove for a time along the narrow streets of the market district, taking sudden turns, and u-turns. Only when satisfied they were not followed, he drove out of town, into the countryside.

"Where we going?" Dorn asked.

"I'd like to show you something."

Dorn shot a telling look at his wristwatch.

"It won't be a waste of time. It may even aid you in your mission," Brother Anselm said with a particular intonation.

24. Los Vampiros

Intrigued, Dorn watched the zigzagged road as it wound its way past villages and fields, to a spectacular vista of a sun-drenched valley dominated by a massive volcano. After a while they turned off the highway and followed an unmarked dirt road toward a copse of cypresses. Hidden among the tall trees was a church spire, and ruins of a convent bathing in sunlight. No person was in sight as they pulled into a shaded area along the wall of what once was a cemetery.

"An ex-convent of the Dominican sisters," Brother Anselm said as they strolled along the wall. "Abandoned after the Order's expulsion, it was used as army barracks, and when the military moved out it was looted for the building material."

"Why was the church spared?" Dorn looked up to the spire, which appeared untouched by the tides of history.

"Unlike the convent, it was not raised directly over the ancient Pipil ceremonial site."

They reached a breach in the wall and stopped. To one side stood the church, to the other the ruins, and directly ahead a distant mountain range. Brother Anselm pointed toward the latter.

"You can imagine the size of the convent when you consider that virtually every household from here to the mountains was raised using the stone looted from the site."

"Not unusual for this part of the world," Dorn commented sententiously.

He wondered why Brother Anselm drove him all the way to give a tour of the site, but one look into his mentor's eyes told him to expect the punch line. He followed the elderly's gaze to a path, which wound its way alongside the church structure and disappeared into the barrens. Dorn realized they were waiting for something, or someone, and he had better remain patient.

"The church returned eventually?" Dorn asked to help pass the time.

"Of course the church returned. One can remove a people, or destroy a building, but one cannot wipe out what the building stands for, and what the people believe in."

"Yet the church was raised on an old pagan site to make the locals embrace a new set of beliefs—" Dorn suggested contrarily.

"If only! Alas, Spanish steel was used to convert the peoples. Perhaps because of the steel the aboriginals did not entirely give up their old customs and beliefs. Who knows what would have been had the conquest been left to the missionaries who carried the cross instead of a sword? The fact the people here worship Jesus alongside their ancient Spirits, only speaks to the power of His love—"

"How do you reconcile it with the dismantled convent?"

"Tides of history. The nuns were expelled, but the Church returned eventually, in the person of a lone priest, who brought confirmation to rumors of buried treasures—"

Dorn raised his brows, but said nothing.

Brother Anselm continued, "The priest was authorized to settle an old dispute with the elders. An agreement was drawn. The descendants of the Pipils were made the guardians of the church paraphernalia, and as a good gesture their ancestors' artifacts, stolen during the conquest, were returned to them. The treasures were unearthed, and none too late. The revolution broke out. The military arrived and turned the convent into barracks. The insurgents drove the soldiers out, and the people destroyed the site in part from hatred of the dictatorship, and in part because of poverty. The stone was an excellent building material."

The bell tower struck the hour, its unexpected sound breaking the musings brought about by the mysterious history of the site.

"It works!" Dorn said with amazement.

Brother Anselm smiled.

"Come, I want you to meet someone."

They approached the ornately carved gate, and Brother Anselm used the old iron knocker. The gate opened shortly and a man of native features smiled at Brother Anselm. They embraced as two old friends, and exchanged quick words in the local dialect. Dorn could not understand the words, but no words were necessary to see the extreme reverence Brother Anselm was held in by the native man.

"This is Juan," Brother Anselm introduced.

They followed the man inside, and Dorn was soon overwhelmed by the smell of burned candles, incense, and wood polish.

"Juan is the grounds keeper here. He's been taking care of the church for nearly two decades. He's also a good story teller. He has many to tell. It is from him I learned the history of this place."

They crossed the altar, and entered the sacristy, where it was brighter due to a set of low lying windows. Brother Anselm said several words to their guide, and without much ado the man lifted his blouse, exposing a big scar.

Dorn looked at the scar, then at Juan, and at last at Brother Anselm. He did not understand.

His friend held the shirt higher, and invited Dorn for a closer look.

It was a crude job, the sutures uneven, reminiscent of a poor tailoring job made by a child at a summer camp.

"What is the meaning of this?" Dorn asked.

"Years ago Juan and his wife Nayeli were living in a small shack at the foothills of the mountains. One day a truck arrived in the small hamlet. Several men and women dressed in white robes claimed to represent a charitable foundation. They said they came to distribute free medications and to offer free checkups. They set up on the main square and proceeded to conduct a variety of basic tests. The elderly did not participate, but the young did, and among them were Juan and Nayeli.

"Some weeks later the truck pulled up in front of Juan's home, and he and his wife were abducted, dragged away in the middle of the night. Juan doesn't remember what happened next. He woke up among the ruins of the ex-convent, terrible pain at his side. He was bandaged but bleeding. He passed out. When he came to again some women tended to him in the church. He learned his kidney had been removed, but it was nothing compared with the loss of his wife who did not survive the removal of both kidneys, and a liver."

"Jesus—" Dorn swept his eyes with the palm of his hand.

Brother Anselm continued mercilessly, "The priest called the police. They came, and then they left, but not before issuing threats to Juan, ostensibly calling it the case of voluntary organ sale gone wrong."

"Did he go to the authorities?"

"The authorities?" Brother Anselm's brows arched. "He was lucky he wasn't beaten, or else he would not have survived. Besides, Juan did not speak any Spanish, like so many natives who refused to assimilate the language of the conqueror."

"The priest! Why did the priest not do more?"

"The priest protested and was beaten. He too was lucky he wasn't killed. Remember this happened during the civil war."

Dorn had witnessed his share of horrors, yet he could not hide the effect of the shocking story, the presence of the victim making it close, personal. His question arose not out of disbelief, but for the lack of other words.

"How can you trust it wasn't a voluntary donation? In this part of the world where the dollar goes a very long way? —"

Juan understood the reference to compensation. With his deep dark eyes on Dorn's, he cried, "No, *señor*! No *dolores*!"

Dolores. Misery. The misery was so intrinsically tied to the history of these peoples it showed even in the nuanced way with which they pronounced the unattainable, the misery-drenched necessity that were dollars. Dorn dropped his eyes.

"Have you brought your camera?" Brother Anselm asked seemingly nonsensically.

Dorn reached into his pocket, and extracted his smartphone.

"Go ahead, point it at Juan."

Dorn did as asked. He knew what would happen, but did not see a correlation.

As expected, Juan turned his back to the lens.

"These people believe a part of them is taken away with every picture. Do you honestly think they'd voluntarily give up their organs?" Brother Anselm did not wait for a reply, and continued, "The locals call them *los vampiros de los órganos*. They arrive under cover of darkness, snatch a person, or an entire family, and disappear into the night. The next morning the abducted wake up in some remote area, an abandoned mining town, a railway station, or a factory, along with others, all screaming in pain, bleeding, rudimentary bandages falling off. No one knows who the vampires are, where they come from, where they go, or who their clients are—"

"The police?" Dorn asked in a weak voice.

"In times of war the police is not a service to turn to for help, not when one's people are the target of the regime's attack."

Brother Anselm knew what question mounted in his friend's mind, Dorn's hesitation to ask it the result of emotional shock.

"You are wondering why I brought you here, to hear this tragic story? I think you know the answer. It goes back to *La Escuela*..."

"*La Escuela*," Dorn repeated numbly. "The School of the Assassins!"

Dorn knew the infamous facility. Rare was a day when, on his way to the Building, he would not encounter protesters who demanded the closing of the school that trained military officers of allied countries, as well as saboteurs and terrorists in countries perceived as hostile. These were the days when he was ashamed of the uniform, the days when he wanted to shout out the window of his car in support of the protesters, "I am a soldier, and I am with you!" Dorn was not naïve, though. He knew a world without armies was not possible, not when boundaries, languages, cultures, affluence, natural resources, poverty, and a myriad other reasons were exploited to espouse nationalistic sympathies and the belief in one's own dominance over others. Militaries were needed by the bullies, and by the bullied. It was a vicious circle. Dorn understood this much, and he never accepted military service as a tool of oppression. He despised the forces, which used the military to further their aggressive agendas. *La Escuela* was part of the system used to foment unrest and division, it maintained conditions in which militaries were on the rise, in ever growing demand. Dorn joined the forces for change to help create a world where the trend would reverse, and stop eventually.

Brother Anselm turned to Juan, and said several words. The native's face expressed hope, his glowing eyes on Dorn.

What hope can still exist for this man, when nothing could bring back Nayeli? Dorn wondered. He listened as the two spoke quickly in the incomprehensible language. He watched them embrace, and then he followed his friend outside. Before the gate closed behind them, Dorn turned around to meet the glowing eyes firmly set on his.

The two crossed the dusty stretch of earth to the trees, and approached the old wall, where Brother Anselm found a stone to sit on, and stretched his old legs into the sun. He massaged his kneecaps and sighed. Shifting his body to allow more sun on his sore limbs, he said with an uneasy smile, "Guilty pleasure. Doctors say I ought to avoid the sun. It feels so good, though. It is a paradise, here. Paradise drenched in misery. It ought not surprise, though. Where there are people there is pain. From the stone ages through the Vandal invasions, to your own Civil War, and all wars that followed, one of the unwritten prerogatives of a conqueror, however objectionable and morally reprehensible the practice, was and is looting. It is, as some would have it, a part of warfare itself."

Dorn did not sit down. He was pacing back and forth.

"But how does one go from looting to organ snatching?" he asked irritably, his voice hoarse, his throat dry.

Brother Anselm replied with his eyes closed, his face to the sun, "I suppose it depends how you define treasure? As something, which someone finds valuable? Something unattainable, perhaps? For one it may be love. For someone else something more temporal — an object of art, or gems, or money, or some such traditional riches. For someone else a life-prolonging body organ— No, no! Do not cringe! Harvesting organs during armed conflicts is well documented throughout history, from times immemorial, where tribes extracted their enemies' hearts in belief their consumption would strengthen the victors. But we do not need to turn to anthropological science for examples. Throughout modern times, as medical science grew, people turned to the battlefields as source of human organs, for research, or otherwise."

"But what good is a dead organ?" Dorn wiped the sweat off his forehead and neck with the sleeve of his shirt, not at all certain his perspiration was caused by the sun at its zenith alone.

"No everyone dies in combat, and a battlefield seems an ideal place to harvest organs. With the number of the missing, it is, basically, a crime with impunity. Just ask Foras Helborn—"

Dorn stiffened.

"Helborn? How does he fit into it?"

"Helborn was a military medic. His service record shows he served during every military intervention, including the last civil war that ravaged this poor country."

"What are you suggesting?" Dorn embraced his face with his glistening hands.

"Organ transplantation is a very lucrative business, like any business where demand surpasses supply. Lack of donors, or legislative restrictions, create a situation, which leads to desperation. The desperate who can afford it will pay dearly."

"Are you suggesting that organ snatching is organized?"

Brother Anselm's eyes opened and centered on Dorn.

"Worse. It is institutionalized."

"How can it be? You have been to a warfront. You've seen what it's like when one's own troops can hardly receive proper treatment. How can something as sophisticated as organ harvesting take place in such conditions?"

"We are living is an era when wars are fought by private armies. These are units which invade, kill, rape, and rob solely for profit. Dealing in human organs is only a small part of their business."

"But I still fail to understand how it is made possible, at all? Removing a kidney, or a liver, is not something easily accomplished in a combat situation, not to mention the need for proper storage and transportation."

"These private armies have access to military bases and facilities—"

"The military bases?" Dorn asked in awe.

"Don't be surprised, such trade can be made possible only with institutionalized support."

Dorn took time to absorb the news. He had seen pain, and he had witnessed misery. This was only one more example of a world in desperate need of change.

He unbuttoned his shirt entirely, took it off, and used it to fan himself.

"How did Helborn come to know Kachem?"

The answer was given immediately, as though Brother Anselm expected the question.

"Kachem was an instructor at *La Escuela*, where he trained the contras and death squads. The staff came from all walks of life, including medical teams. One of the military doctors was a surgeon by the name Foras Helborn…"

"Why is he here now?" he asked through his teeth.

"Helborn was discharged from the military. He now works with the private contractors, but he is here on a matter unrelated to both. He's here after the ancient treasures. He must have learned of them from his victims."

25. The Warning

The drive to the city was a gloomy affair despite beautiful vistas. The same views, earlier in the day, imbued Dorn with happy prospects, as though looking far into a closing horizon, he was glancing into an approaching better future. This time a brighter future seemed ever more distant, unattainable. It felt as though for every good deed done by people such as Brother Anselm, twofold as many were committed by the likes of Foras Helborn. The meeting of Juan reminded Dorn of the day when he first self-realized his desire to commit to change. Always energetic, preferring action to study, having barely passed the seminary exams, Dorn welcomed the opportunity to participate in fieldwork, and put action into words. His work at the infirmary offered semblance of a meaningful service for change, but it turned out only to cure the effects of the evil he wanted to fight. For a meaningful change one ought to tackle the causes of evil. He was presented with that opportunity. The torching of the infirmary was the catalyst. It was the moment when something profound changed in Dorn. Barely nineteen, he was but a boy, mature perhaps, but a boy nonetheless. That day he became a man. He vowed to drop the frock, to forgo a scholarly future, to which he felt no necessary drive, and to join the fight in a capacity better suiting his persona. Brother Anselm was the first to see the change in his young protégé, and suggested the course of action — to burrow deep into the very beast, to destroy the conditions, which created the necessity for the infirmary. Dorn was determined to destroy *La Escuela*, that factory of tormentors, and all it stood for. He changed one uniform for another. He enlisted, became a soldier, an intelligence analyst, driven by the dogged desire to bring about change. Now, years later, it seemed he was no closer to achieving his dream. It seemed that for every small success the evil struck with an ever growing pain.

"Brother Anselm, what are we doing wrong?" he opened.

The elderly glanced at him. One look was enough to assess the state of mind of the passenger.

He replied cautiously, "To question is to begin to seek change."

"When change does not come?"

"Change has come."

"I can't see it."

"Perhaps you are looking too far. Look closer, Kamil. Look to yourself. Change is in you. You are it."

Dorn took time to absorb the reply. Brother Anselm was right, but the answer was not satisfying. Who was he but an insignificant young man facing a giant of immeasurable proportions, omnipotent and omnipresent?

The silver-haired angel behind the wheel understood.

"You are not alone. Each day new hearts and minds join the cause because of you, because of others like you. People see the change is possible when they are not alone. You are the force of change. It is because of you, and I mean it both as singular and plural, because of you that such atrocities as the burning of the infirmary, or as the killing of the Fathers of the Universidad, are no longer part of day-to-day business in places such as this. The people see and feel the winds of change are upon."

"I can't help but wonder if the winds can sweep quickly enough!"

"We cannot change overnight what has been tormenting the human race since the beginning of time. We must completely rearrange the foundations of the old world in order to build a new one. Brick by brick, heart by heart, mind by mind, we are getting there. A new, a better world, is possible, and the necessary change is underway. Look at what we've achieved. We've built base communities where the people can create their own futures by taking to trades. We've opened schools where previously none were available. We've started a system of micro-loans, which eliminates the need to enlist big banks — this tool of modern-day slavery. We've taught people to come together, to form a unified force. We've become them, and they've become us. They carry the message we bring to them. You mustn't doubt yourself, Kamil. Evil is still amongst us, but it is in retreat—"

Dorn looked forward through the windshield, and into the horizon. It no longer seemed as dark and unattainable. He saw the light, and it was not merely the sun nearing the apparent meeting place of the sky and the earth. He saw light in his purpose. That it resembled the sun approaching the horizon directly ahead of them, above the highway, was a sign. He rested his eyes on the skyline to feast his mind with the happier thoughts, when his senses told him to beware. He concentrated his eyes. At the distance he saw several vehicles on the side of the road, persons moving about, scouting the passing cars, waving them by. As they neared he could make out assault rifles in the hands of the men. It was too late to turn around, not without raising undue attention.

Dorn had no reasonable cause for alarm, after all road blocks were common in this country on the brink of civil war. The regime sought the revolutionaries, or drug traffickers, depending on the language needed to explain the more and more frequent intrusions resulting in shootings and deaths. Yet he could not help his heart tremble. The armed men waved all vehicles right by, and Dorn's gut was telling him to expect trouble. His suspicions were correct. They were flagged as soon as they neared, and assault rifles were aimed at the vehicle to ensure compliance.

Brother Anselm pulled over.

An officer approached the car, and circled it. He appeared at the driver's side, and commanded in Spanish, "Get out."

Dorn touched Brother Anselm's arm, and opened the door. He stepped out, turned to the officer, and spoke in English, "What is the trouble, officer?"

The soldier dismissed him. His eyes on the driver, he repeated forcefully, "Out of the vehicle, *viejo*!"

Brother Anselm opened the door. He emerged on the side of the road, and stood straight, his eyes on the soldier's.

"What is the meaning of this?" Dorn stepped forward.

Several barrels aimed at his abdomen.

"Beware whom you raise your weapons against!" Brother Anselm cried, his voice hovering over the scene.

His voice startled the soldiers. Unexpected strength reverberated from his every word, permeating under their skulls, touching their hearts.

The officer pointed a finger at one of the two military pick-ups, and motioned Brother Anselm toward it.

The elderly did not move.

Prompted by their officer two soldiers rushed in, their barrels nudging the silver-haired on the back.

"I demand an answer to this!" Dorn raised his voice.

He did not finish, a blow to his solar plexus throwing him to his knees. Gasping for air he watched as the soldiers butted Brother Anselm, ushering him into their vehicle. He had to do something, and do it quickly.

Brother Anselm showed no fear.

"Soldiers! Brothers! Do not listen to those who tell you to kill. Listen instead to the words of God — Thou shalt not kill! Lower your weapons. Speak up against injustice. Blood is on your hands when you say nothing—"

The officer approached him in two quick steps and butted on the occipital.

Brother Anselm stumbled but did not fall. He addressed the soldiers again, "Drop your weapons. Blood is on your hands when you say nothing, when you do nothing! Your only enemy is he who tells you to kill—"

A second blow threw him to the ground.

The officer ordered his soldiers to pick up the old man.

Dorn was desperate. It was clear the purpose of the block was to detain Brother Anselm. Why? He could only speculate, but to speculate he had no time. In seconds Brother Anselm would be gone, and no amount of speculation could help. In an act of desperation, Dorn rose up and threw himself at Brother Anselm as the elderly was passing by, ushered away under the barrels of the guns. The two fell to the ground, Dorn's body covering his friend's. He began to shout. When later asked, he could not recall the exact words, driven by the prevailing thought to submit the soldiers to higher authority, the authority of the Superpower without whose material and logistical support the puppet regime and its military would not spread their evil tentacles as quickly and deeply into the society.

"Stop at once!" he cried in English. He continued in Spanish, "I am an officer with the only power in the world that supports you, and this man is under my protection! I command you! Let us go!"

Dorn outburst had an immediate effect, inasmuch that the soldiers froze, uncertain, their eyes darting between their commanding officer and the Gringo. The officer, too, wavered momentarily.

Dorn clung to the only chance they had. Seeing as the soldiers were undecided, he rose to his feet, and helped Brother Anselm up.

He cried to the others, "We are under the protection of the embassy!"

121

Continuing to shout similar expletives, he withdrew to the car, the soldiers advancing, but daring not act against the Gringo, awaiting instructions. None came, and, with Dorn behind the wheel, the decrepit sedan took off with the squeak of the tires.

26. Unwanted Visitors

The event too fresh, his mind too shaken, Dorn asked no questions, his entire concentration was focused on fleeing the scene. He drove away as quickly as the rattling vehicle permitted, taking frequent glances into the reverse mirror. They were not pursued, but Dorn could not rule out another roadblock ahead. Realizing the tremendous danger, he turned off the highway and decided to return to the capital city via side roads. Thirty minutes later, his tension trailing behind his desire to seek answers, Dorn pulled over.

"It was a close call, Brother Anselm," he said.

Brother Anselm rolled down the window. He gazed into the horizon with the imposing mass of the volcano in front of them. He said nothing.

"It was clear they were waiting for you," Dorn pressed. "Had you been alone they would've— You must disappear."

"Think nothing of it, Kamil. I cannot disappear, as long as injustice does not disappear."

123

"Next time I may not be with you to impose the imperial pressure!"

"We cannot cower. We cannot wait for miracles, not anymore. We must act, even if it means sacrificing ourselves. We are insignificant inasmuch as our mortal coil is concerned. Think nothing of it. What we are a part of is more important. They can take one of us out, they can take us out by the droves, but they can no longer stop what we've started. With or without us our thought will continue. We have become an erupting volcano. Unstoppable."

Dorn sat in silence. What could he offer in retort? He knew Brother Anselm was right. He knew it because he would do the same. Every one of them would offer the same reply. They had committed to change because they were called to it. Each one of them was convinced they were personally called by Him, to become His associates, to join His Company. To cower now would mean to betray Him.

"Is your place safe, at least?" Dorn asked.

"My own safety is insignificant—"

"Brother Anselm!" Dorn protested.

"As safe as is reasonably possible," the elderly said in a pacifying voice. "But let us return to the city. We must carry on."

Dorn drove Brother Anselm to an unassuming hotel where his friend took a room, and returned to the plaza by taxi. Not wanting to encounter Capt. Weader, he took the back entrance, and quickly climbed the stairs to his floor. He opened a bottle of water he bought at a corner *tienda* the previous night, and drank half. It was tepid. He picked up a plastic container from the table, and went out to the hallway, to an ice dispenser. He filled the container, returned to his room, and placed the bottle in it. Waiting for the water to cool, he took a shower. When he came out he was met with a barrel of a pistol aimed at his abdomen.

The two burly men wore tight jeans and loose shirts. Speaking broken English, one of them said, "Put something on."

They added something else between themselves, apparently finding amusement in his stark nakedness.

Dorn did not sense open hostility, rather determination to follow orders. Their rough-cut, wind-blown faces, and muscles bulging through the closely fit trousers discouraged opposition, yet he could think of no alternative to physical confrontation as the only means to regain control of the situation.

Taking advantage of their diverted alertness, Dorn covered his private parts with feigned modesty. The move made the men burst out with laughter. For a split second the one holding the pistol had lowered the barrel as he used his free hand to clap his buddy on the shoulder. Dorn seized the moment. His left foot kicked up, but, to his horror, it barely reached the wrist. While the impact caused the hand to arch upward, the pistol remained in the firm grip. Without delay Dorn lunged forward, his body weight bringing both of them down.

While they struggled for control of the weapon, the second assailant appeared the more amused by the uncommon scene of a naked man crouching over his buddy. In the whirling Dorn managed to jab his middle finger into his opponent's eye. He felt the grip loosen, saw the pistol slide out of the hand, and roll under the bed. He reached for it, and at the same moment his head exploded.

He came to abruptly, shaking his head violently. He found himself seated in a chair, his wrists tied behind his back, his legs strapped to the chair with shoelaces. Water dripped from his chin and tickled his bare chest as it streamed down. He kicked his legs. It was in vain. His ankles were tied to chair legs. The blood made his temples throb the more.

He coughed when a stream of water hit his head, pouring into his nose, choking him. He opened his eyes, and gasped for air at the sight of the man who towered over him, a bucket of water in his hands.

"It didn't have to turn this unpleasant, if only you listened to me," Chief Jorge del Toro said in English, his face still, cut in stone.

Dorn said nothing, unable to utter a word even if he wanted to. His mouth was gagged. It became evident when he tried to catch a breath, his nostrils stuffed with water. He blew his nose till most of the water escaped. Breathing hard, and sweating despite the cold water, he envisioned himself strapped to the chair, all naked, and gagged. He could not help but burst out a silent laughter. His shoulders shaking from the nervous laughter, his eyes struggled to conceal overwhelming anxiety.

The chief said, his eyes sharp and cruel, "I'm going to make an example of you."

27. Persuasive Arguments

The killer from the Sierra Madres flicked his fingers, and the gesture set his two sidekicks in motion. One picked up the floor lamp, unplugged it from the receptacle, and placed the plug under his foot. One jerk broke the cord, exposing two wires. He proceeded to separate the wires by pulling them apart, stripping the insulation. He inserted the plug into the receptacle and, holding the exposed copper wires in an outstretched arm, he squinted while his eyes glided over Dorn's wet and naked body. Meanwhile the second of the thugs appeared on the side of the chair with a fresh bucket of water, and a grin of expected pleasure on his lean and cruel face.

Chief del Toro looked down, and said, "I'm going to ask you some questions. Answer yes by blinking once, or no by not blinking. Do not shake your head. Do not hesitate with your response. Understood?"

Dorn blinked.

"Are you here in an official capacity?" del Toro shot straight from the shoulder.

Dorn blinked.

"Will you tell me why you are here?"

Dorn kept his eyes open.

The Chief expected no other answer and proceeded without a flinch, "Is the embassy aware of your mission?"

Dorn kept his eyes open despite water dripping from his wet hair and tingling his pupils.

"Is it a black operation, then?"

Dorn blinked. It was an involuntary reaction, caused by the water. He blinked several times, until his eyes filled with tears. His lids closed.

"Are you here alone?" the Chief pried on. Not receiving a response, he continued with more questions. "Will you tell me what your mission entails? … Tell me the name of you commanding officer?"

Seeing as no cooperation was forthcoming, he straightened and gestured to his sidekicks.

Water poured onto Dorn's exposed testicles, and streamed down to his feet. He opened his eyes just as the thug with the cord approached and the exposed wires neared the groin.

"Tell me what you're doing here?" del Toro offered him another chance.

Dorn closed his eyes in expectation of the worst. He was prepared to die a martyr. He knew the killer was not uttering empty threats. He had seen the smoking barrel in his hands that fateful day, and he knew no amount of pleading would do. He knew men like del Toro, graduates of *La Escuela* — brutal and unscrupulous, often deranged henchmen, who studied the art of torturous interrogation. It was the latter realization, which helped Dorn to take heart and gave him an idea. *La Escuela's* purpose was to train forces for the battle against domestic opposition, revolutionaries, insurgents, and fomenters of change — the Company, the biggest threat, according to the Junta. Protecting the Company, and completing the mission was thus paramount. Sacrificing himself today was not written in his books, and Dorn opened his eyes. He blinked.

"You wanna talk, amigo?" del Toro watched him closely.

Dorn blinked.

"Will you scream when I remove the gag?"

Dorn's eyes remained open, his heart rushed as he kept on staring into the cold eyes of his tormentor.

Chief del Toro signaled his men. The one with the electric cord remained in place, while the other untangled the knot, and extracted the gag from the captive's mouth — a piece of cloth, Dorn's own underwear.

"Talk, amigo," Del Toro encouraged sweetly.

***

No particular skills at reading micro-expressions were required to realize Dorn had hit the spot.

Chief del Toro's face turned white in an instant, his breath slowed down. His back straightened, giving the impression of the officer doubling in size.

"What did you say?" he asked.

In his predicament Dorn came up with the only answer, which came to mind. It was a gamble, but it worked, and the effect it caused surpassed any expectations.

Dorn repeated, "The Building has been infiltrated by the Company. I was sent here to stop them."

The killer pondered the answer in silence, his eyes nailed to Dorn's. He took the sunglasses out of his shirt and wiped the lenses, seemingly absentmindedly.

"You've come to battle the Company?" he asked at last, his hands busy with the specs.

"Your enemy is my enemy."

The Chief's gaze weighed on him for a long time.

"Then why did you not come to us straight away?"

"You never know who's who."

Del Toro snorted, but in the swaggering gesture Dorn detected permeating sense of insecurity. He was on the right track, and it was time to hit harder.

"You've allowed the Company to build a stronghold in your country," he said condescendingly.

The officer's face turned tamarillo and then reverted to raw tortilla. He grinned and bit back, "If it wasn't for your blindsided war on terror, and diversion of resources, we'd have carried out the final solution long time ago!"

It took the thousands of invisible souls working as one to give Dorn the strength not to show the emotional effect of the killer's statement. He stared the huge man in the eyes in a classic example of *reservatio mentalis*, so often so successfully employed by so many Jesuits who found themselves in dire straights. He gathered his strength through the channeling of his core convictions, and he backed up his claim by amplifying the Company's growing worldwide influence.

"Your home-grown priests have sparked a global revolution. The calls to rise up, to overthrow the established political and banking systems, and to destroy the military-industrial complexes, it all originates here—"

"We've been warning you about this for years," the Chief said incredulously. "Why the hell do you think we tried to overthrow the neighboring government, if not to rid its parliament of red priests? And what the hell did we receive in response? You scolded us on the international scene!"

"Our politicians are blind. They may even be under Jesuit influence. This is where I come in, to put an end to the Company, as you started when you took out the Six."

Though he could not guess the Chief's full role in the events, Dorn thought his words played to the killer's psyche when he alluded to the murder of the six priests, the University professors. He was not mistaken.

Chief del Toro hung a long gaze on Dorn.

"You have woken up, at last," he said.

Dorn pressed on, aware how precarious was his position, "We do not have the ability to act as freely as you do, in your country. We are a democracy. Our military's hands are tied by civilians who do not understand the need to strike before the enemy grows too strong. We ought to act now, and eradicate the threat before they drag the world into an all-out war. We can no longer wait while the politicians squabble. This is the final whistle to act."

The Chief nodded appreciatively.

"What is your plan?"

"You are forcing me to tell what I am not authorized to reveal."

"We are allies, are we not?"

"Very well," Dorn replied after due silence, and he told the officer about the courier and the mole.

Jorge del Toro showed no surprise.

"Is one of them the priest you were seen with today?" he asked simply.

Dorn swallowed hard.

"No harm should come to either," he replied noncommittally.

"Why?"

"It is part of the black op, to carry out the... final solution. As brutal as it sounds, it's a delicate operation. You know the Company has eyes and ears everywhere. Besides, we must care about the reverberations such an act will have on global scale. My country is already the most despised in the world—"

The chief studied his face for a long time.

"The world despises you because you've become weak. Were you stronger you would not care what the world thinks."

"Politicians!" Dorn snorted.

The Chief watched him closely, and smiled appreciatively.

"Your politicians could learn something from ours." He projected big predatory teeth, and added, "What do you intend next?"

"How about getting out of these shackles."

Del Toro signaled his men. The two proceeded to untie Dorn. Freed, covered with a towel, he moved unhurriedly about the room. He found his water bottle, slowly unscrewed the cap, and drank.

"You must not do anything, which might alert the courier," he said at last.

"What about the final solution?" the Chief asked.

"It will happen by itself."

The officer looked at him doubtfully.

Their eyes sparred. Dorn stared back at the killer despite his heart pounding in uncertainty.

"Alright, amigo. I'm sure your strategists thought out the best tactic," the officer said. "Remember we can help when something goes wrong. We are allies, after all."

Dorn mustered all the strength he could to calm himself after del Torro and his bullies left the room. The encounter left him shaken beyond his ability to quash its effects by summoning *reservatio mentalis*. He felt lonely, a tiny speck of a waning light in the dark sea of evil. On the verge of losing whatever sanity allowed him to remain in control of his senses he kicked up his leg, then the other, and engaged in an kickboxing fight with a nonexistent enemy whose face he saw clearly in front of his eyes, his fists reaching the mark, turning it into a bloody pulp. He continued thus, his limbs cutting the air, until exhaustion made his knees tremble. He then sank to the floor and wept.

28. A Shot in the Dark

The recently revamped Arena Park marked the northeast boundary of the Centro Histórico. Located at the confluence of residential and commercial districts, the large wooded park was circled by a busy road. It was poorly lit, with but a few lampposts, and most illumination was provided indirectly from rundown residences across the streets. During daytime the park offered the much-needed shade for sun-beaten residents; after sundown it attracted lovers of all ages who appreciated the soundproof canopy of dense brush. Several large fountains were scattered around the park, one in each corner, whereas the largest one occupied the central point. Water in the fountains was yellow-brown from rusted water mains, but at night it whispered romantically for the couples who occupied the area in tight embraces, its color open to imagination. At a distance street vendors sold sugar candy, balloons, sodas, churros, and cheap plastic jewelry. Dorn appreciated Fink's choice, as the place offered relative privacy, and the ease of disappearance into the dark. He was late for the meeting because of the encounter with Chief del Toro and the mind-cleansing walk he required afterwards. The thirty minutes trotted along the exhaust-ridden main thoroughfare did help to calm his senses and suppress the immediate desire to confront the killer, to do onto him what he and his henchmen did to the patients of the infirmary.

He arrived in the park still shaken, but ready to face the next stage in the battle for a world without men such as del Toro. He circled the central fountain to allow his eyes to adjust to darkness. With only young couples in the vicinity he was beginning to worry, when he heard rustle in the shadows of a thicket behind a line of park benches.

Out of the thick shrubbery emerged Chad Fink.

The two men studied one another at close proximity, the only available source of illumination reaching them from a distant building, its windows casting glimmers of faint reflections on each face.

"The courier has arrived," Fink broke the silence. The snitch was wearing a bomber jacket, with both hands in its pockets. Before Dorn could reply, Fink added in a voice laced with an icy undertone that felt as though a cold blade was jabbing into the other man's chest, "The mole is here too."

Dorn shivered. He thanked the providence for the meeting taking place in darkness, lest his face reveal what went on in his mind.

"Do you have the information I came for?" he demanded in a brusque tone he hoped would conceal his emotional strain and project authority.

"It is why I am here. To help rid my country of traitors. Isn't it your job, too, Pvt. Dorn?"

Fink's persistent holding of his hands in his coat pockets and exhibiting hostile attitude was unnerving.

"Is your information reliable?"

"I told you I'm good at what I do," Fink went on. "I deliver solid gold."

Alarms rang in Dorn's head.

"What are you sources?" he asked.

Fink snorted.

"Do you think I'd've survived here this long if I gave away my operational secrets?"

"How do I know your information is accurate?"

"Have I ever given your employers a reason to doubt my sources?"

Dorn was losing ground. The cryptic replies left no doubt in his mind the snitch possessed information, which exposed Dorn, but where did he acquire it from?

"Your sources are reliable?" he asked, repeating himself.

"The best," Fink was toying with him

The tenser Dorn's voice grew, the cockier was Fink's.

"Let's have it then, man!" Dorn was at a last straw. He knew his anxiety was evident, he could hear it in his own voice, but he disregarded it, driven now by the sole desire to extract the information he wanted. "Where is he?"

"The courier, or the mole?" Fink grinned, in the darkness the contraction giving his face an eerie appearance. Having not received a reply, he went on, "The courier is hiding at a hacienda outside the city, but the mole— The mole is closer — Much closer—" Fink paused abruptly and turned to face the thicket behind his back.

Dorn heard it too. It must have been Brother Anselm, and he welcomed the distraction. He reached into the small of his back, his hand embracing the handle of a knife he swiped from a table of the hotel restaurant. He stood sideways to Fink hoping the move went unnoticed. He kept his guard, the firm grip on the handle giving him the necessary, if false confidence to prowl for more information.

His fortune changed in an instant when his eye registered a glistening object in Fink's hand.

Dorn panicked. As he drew out his knife, he heard a muted thump followed by a gurgling sound. He saw the snitch spin around and slump onto the ground. The thicket, which drew Fink's attention, began to move and rustling sounds turned into sounds of struggle. Moments later Dorn heard quick footsteps disappear into the darkness of the park. A coughing sound that followed belonged to a person in peril. Dorn rushed toward the source of the sound. He found the elderly man on the ground, behind a trunk of a tree.

"Brother Anselm!"

The man struggled to his feet as Dorn approached, his breath labored.

"They took me by surprise— I saw a flash, heard a muffled shot— We struggled— Solar plexus—" Brother Anselm spat out the words as he gasped for air.

"Are you shot?" Dorn asked.

"No, but Fink— Is he?—"

They crossed the park alley where Fink lay on the ground, his arms twisted unnaturally. Dorn felt for pulse. He detected none. He felt about the body. The snitch's fingers were grasping an object, which earlier Dorn took for a weapon. It was a pack of cigarettes, its cellophane packaging reflecting flicks of light.

"Did you hear everything?"

"Most," Brother Anselm confirmed.

"You think he knew who the mole is?"

"He would've come armed if he did."

The logic of it was inescapable, yet with the snitch's voice still fresh in his ears, Dorn could not help but wonder why such vehement assurance in professing to know the identity of the mole?

"What about the courier? The hacienda out of town? Sound familiar?"

"I think I know the place," Brother Anselm said. "But we must go now. Come, you shouldn't be seen here."

They walked briskly toward the lights of the street. Brother Anselm was quickly recovering from the blow, and Dorn was coming to from the numbness caused by the unexpected turn of events.

"Who do you think Fink's sources are?" Dorn asked over his shoulder.

"MORT," was the immediate reply.

"Who?"

"MORT. The state's network of snitches and informants. Created under the military dictatorship, they number in tens — if not hundreds of thousands. The MORT informants are present in every organization and community. Some say they are in every family."

"Family?"

"Don't be surprised. The STASI did it, too. People are paid or coerced to report on their neighbors, employers, or family members. Those who take up spying out of conviction or for monetary rewards are assured a better life in this poverty-stricken nation. MORT members are awarded jobs and privileges, which make them ideologically and financially tied to the Junta. It is possible they managed to penetrate the Invisible Company, learn the courier's hideout. It means we ought to go to the hacienda immediately."

They passed the deserted Mercado, a halfway point between the Arena Park and the Plaza Catedral, and Dorn picked up his pace.

"It has to wait," he said under his breath.

"It oughtn't!" Brother Anselm protested.

"But Fink's death—"

"Oh, he probably dug too deep into MORT. Someone became uncomfortable, and—"

"I don't buy it. It's a little too coincidental for a man who managed to remain undetected for so many years to fall so suddenly," Dorn replied between breaths.

"He must've been suspected, watched, or— Somebody was watching you, and followed—"

"Perhaps," Dorn said in a distant voice. "Perhaps that someone was already waiting—"

Brother Anselm said nothing. He awaited clarification.

"There is someone who knew about my meeting with Fink—" Dorn explained.

"You don't think that I—"

The sound of Brother Anselm's voice made Dorn stop in place.

"No, of course not!" he said. "Your devotion to the cause is beyond doubt. It is not you I had in mind." He did not expound on his thought any further and resumed his walk.

"Wait," Brother Anselm struggled to keep pace. "What did you mean?"

Dorn did not reply. They were nearing the Plaza Catedral.

"Kamil," Brother Anselm tried again when the flow of passersby thinned around them. "We ought to go to the hacienda!"

It would not be. Dorn could not postpone what seemed a priority of the moment: finding out the whereabouts of the only other person who knew about his meeting with Chad Fink. He requested an hour's time, and the two agreed to meet at Brother Anselm's hotel. They parted without a word.

Anxious to reach the hotel room located directly below his, Dorn did not notice the two shadows who followed his friend.

29. Surprise

Dorn had to know. He climbed the staircase instead of waiting for the old-fashioned and slow elevator. Rather than fumble with the lock picks, which might alert the occupant, he rushed into his room, and onto the balcony. He leaned over the railing and looked down. The third floor did not seem high in the darkness. The tall Indian laurel tree provided additional cover from the prying eyes, and without further ado he swung hid legs over the railing and onto the ledge. With his hands grasping the rails, he let his feet down until they felt the railing below.

The balcony door was ajar, the drapes swaying in a gentle breeze. Capt. Weader was not home, and Dorn proceeded to scout her room. Hollie was an organized woman, her belongings neatly folded and kept in the suitcase — a wise choice for someone in need of a hasty departure. Nothing was thrown on the floor or scattered on the furniture. The only objects in the lavatory were a toothbrush, a toothpaste, and a comb. The woman's neatness was a detriment, requiring particular set of skills, an eye to detail, and an equally organized mind when undetected pillage was desired. Invisible traps could be anywhere.

Dorn started with the suitcase, going through it methodically, feeling every garment and every item. He then turned his attention to the wardrobe, and went on to upturn the mattress. Having found nothing he unloaded his frustration on the trash bin, throwing its contents — bills and airline baggage tags — onto the bed. He did not know what he was looking for, and he found nothing to support his suspicions.

He exhaled deeply, and sat down on the bed to think for a minute. Perhaps he was wrong? Why would Weader want to kill Fink, anyway? The two of them represented the same side. But if not the woman, then who? Could Chief del Toro have found out about the meeting? Even so it was unlikely he'd kill the snitch for in the end they both worked against the Company. This left the woman, the only other person with foreknowledge of the meeting.

Dorn did not find proof, but his hunch was telling him he was on the right track. In his mind it was only a matter of finding the link. It seemed a direct confrontation with the woman was inevitable, and with it a possible exposure of his own identity, unless— He was struck with a sudden idea. Perhaps he could find out what really happened, and not expose himself?

Dorn jumped to his feet, and picked up the suitcase. He threw all its contents onto the bed, mixing everything together. He took a step back, and smiled. This ought to unseat the woman, a reaction he could turn into his advantage. Hopeful, he approached the door, and unlocked it in order to suggest the way burglars entered the room. At the same time the handle turned and Capt. Weader appeared in the doorway.

They observed one another for a time.

"Fink has been shot," Dorn said simply.

She did not move, and said nothing.

A middle-aged couple appeared at the end of the hallway, nearing the two officers.

Dorn opened the door wide, stepped aside and waved the woman in.

If Dorn had any doubts before they were now put to flight when Capt. Weader hesitated a moment. Her eyes darted from Dorn to the approaching couple, and he used the opportunity to look her over. Her clothes — a torn blouse, which she attempted to cover with a wide shawl, and a dirty patch on her knee, along with the messy hair — completed the image which convinced Dorn he was right.

Capt. Weader made a decision, and took a step forward. She entered the room brazenly.

Dorn closed the door behind them. He did not switch on the light.

The woman ignored the mess, though she could not have missed it even in the dim light, the only source of which was a crack in the window drapes.

"Who else knew about your meeting with Fink?" she asked reluctantly, the question unavoidable.

"Only three people knew about it. One of them is dead."

He thought her face blushed, but it could have been a flicker of light.

She ignored the biting remark, and shot one in return.

"Perhaps you were followed? All these rancheros look alike, making it hard to spot a shadow—"

He felt blood rush to his face. Capt. Weader connected the passenger from the flight with the man she saw Dorn with in the church, but she did not make and overt accusation. Why? Why was she playing? His mind raced, but he could think of no answer.

"You don't trust me," she said, and cast a sweeping look about the room.

Dorn was puzzled. It was the second time she said it in as many days.

A knock on the door startled both.

"In the bathroom, quick!" she whispered.

He hesitated.

"We're not officially together, remember?" she persisted.

Something in her voice told him she was not deceiving. He withdrew into the bathroom and, his hand gripping the knife handle in his pocket, he watched through a crack between the door and the frame.

He saw the woman wipe her face with the shawl. He saw her take a deep breath. He saw her open the door.

He did not see the person on the other side. He did not have to. He recognized the voice.

30. Upping the Ante

"Hello, Hollie."

Maj. Will Kachem entered the room without an invitation.

"Will," was a simple reply.

Did Dorn detect trembling in her voice?

"This is a surprise," the woman continued.

Is it? Dorn wished he could see her face.

"Is it?" Kachem asked in his trademark confrontational tone.

In that instant Dorn understood what hid behind Hollie's repeated concern over trust. Maj. Kachem's suspicious nature planted a seed of doubt in the woman's mind. The realization brought considerable relief, and for the first time he congratulated himself for being a part of the notorious Major's team, a tribe in the mysterious machine dubbed far and wide as C-*KGB*-IFA. Maj. Hollie Weader, a highly accomplished officer, was stricken with guilt. It could only mean her conscience was not as clear as her accomplishments would have it.

"It needn't be," Kachem went on with a trace of sarcasm.

His nose sniffing, his shifty eyes registering every detail in the room, and ending on the sconce on the wall, Kachem reached for the light switch. His eyes swept the room again, and rested on the woman's.

"How's your progress?" he asked.

"There have been obstacles," the woman said.

In her words Dorn sensed a disconnect between the two officers.

"We have met obstacles," Dorn seconded as he stepped out from the dark bathroom, his voice sounding artificial, out of place.

Kachem looked at the woman, then the man, the dark doorway, and said as though he expected to find Dorn in the bathroom, "Oh?"

Dorn avoided the woman's eyes when he said, "Fink found out who the mole is, and was killed."

Kachem seemed genuinely shocked but, contrary to his character, he did not fume in response to the disappointing news.

Dorn described the circumstances of his meeting with Fink, omitting only Brother Anselm's part.

"Fink's death is a serious blow from a strategic point, but it proves we are close." Kachem's comment came with unbecoming thoughtfulness on his face.

Dorn could not decide whether the officer's words were a mere attempt at philosophizing or a veiled threat. In his guilty mind he read the change in the notorious spy-catcher's tone the only way he could in the circumstances, and Kachem's sudden arrival became an extension of Fink's not so subtle accusation. Did the snitch share his suspicions with the Major?

"What brings you here?" he asked.

"Headquarters is very concerned. The Secretary is pressing to resolve this case as quickly as possible, and you've just suffered a setback." He turned to the woman, and said, "Hollie? Tell me you've at least made contact—"

She blushed, but replied quickly, too quickly, "No."

Dorn looked into her eyes. She avoided his. She was lying, but why? It could only mean that Capt. Weader advanced in the agenda Kachem spoke of on the way to the airport. The cursed inter-agency rivalry filled Dorn with hope. Whatever the untold between Kachem and Weader, it meant a point for Dorn. It meant he could pitch one against the other to further his own mission. He smiled in his mind. Three persons with three agendas stood in the room facing each other. All three held different pieces to the puzzle that brought them together. If he played his part right he could succeed in his assignment and still carry his head out of it in one piece.

He said to up the ante, "I do have a lead, though."

Kachem pricked his ears.

"Tell me!"

"Before he was killed Fink gave away the courier's hideaway."

The woman stiffened.

"Spell it out, man!" Kachem was losing patience.

They both looked at him with expectancy, and Dorn could not help but wonder why Hollie's face turned white. Kachem was right, Dorn thought. Capt. Weader's mission included an agenda that was not shared with the CIFA, perhaps even contrary to its objectives. What was it? Observing the woman's behavior brought him to the one and only logical conclusion: If the CIFA's objective was to pass on the Trojan Horse and allow the courier to carry it back to the Company's headquarters, then Capt. Weader's contrary mission would have to lead to a contrary resolution. It meant that the courier's life was in danger. It mean that Dorn ought to have prioritized better and accompanied Brother Anselm to the hacienda mentioned by the dead man.

31. Waking Dream

In his mind Dorn found confirmation of the woman's hand in the killing of the snitch. Suspecting her unspoken agenda behind the move, he made a skillful excuse and left the two officers under pretext of verifying his information. He only wished it was not too late. Wary of surveillance he took extraordinary precautions in employing every known technique learned from the Escape and Evasion course, further enhanced by field experience, though minor it was, to lose possible pursuers. It took longer, but the caution was necessary. He arrived at Brother Anselm's base late, but certain of not bringing along unwanted guests.

As in many places in the world, a marketplace that supplied the less affluent populace was a good location for one seeking inexpensive and less restrictive accommodation. Hotels in such areas often lacked the facilities to use credit cards, and seldom required other forms of identification, which served well those who preferred anonymity to comfort. The hotel Brother Anselm picked based on this criteria was located a block from the Mercado, attracting vendors and shoppers alike. Some of the former were closing the last of their mobile stalls, and street cleaners appeared here and there with their besoms.

The two-story venue was locked and dark, with no signs of life, and Dorn did not want to draw attention to himself by making a ruckus at the door. He followed the length of the building, looking for additional entry points, but found none, and after brief contemplation he settled on a lamppost, which towered over an awning of a neighboring shop. He assessed the construction solid enough, and used the lamppost to climb on top of it. He ascended quickly to the roof, and from there he leaped over three electrified wires to the terraced roof of the hotel. Navigating between long unused and decaying rooftop furniture he found the staircase to the inner courtyard, the center of which was furnished with restaurant tables. The courtyard was encircled by two-storied balconies lined with guestrooms. Finding number 17 was a breeze, and Dorn started by scratching gently on the door. The lack of answer worried him. He took off his baseball cap and from the rim of the visor he extracted two flat metal wires. The lock gave in not without some struggle, an obstacle cause chiefly by the hardware's age. The room was as shabby on the inside as the hotel was on the outside, and Dorn understood why Brother Anselm had chosen it. It was the sort of place where no undue questions were asked.

With no evidence of a struggle, and all of his friend's belongings neatly organized, Dorn had no reason to suspect foul play in Brother Anselm's absence. He examined the view from the window, where the street was lifeless save for prowling homeless dogs. He then placed an upturned bottle on the door handle, balancing it until it rested against the doorframe without falling, and returned to the bed. He waited in the darkness for his friend's return.

Within minutes he dozed off, but it was not a restful sleep...

He woke up, his heart pounding to the series of deafening explosions accompanied by distant and persistent spats from machine guns. Without having to look out the window he knew the city was under siege. The curfew was no longer observed, and the people set out to the streets to protest the unfair, the unlawful, and dictatorial measures imposed by the Junta. They were met with the only response known to the oppressor, regardless of the geographical location: with fists, boots, clubs, bullets... And bullets flew indiscriminately, for an oppressor sees enemies all around, whether in the guerrillas, the opposition, or ordinary citizens who demand nothing more but to live their lives in peace. An oppressor oppresses the more the greater is the divide that separates him from the population, until he sees nothing but enemies all around, and becomes the enemy to all.

The storming of the University, of what was loudly, if falsely, dubbed the hub of the counterinsurgency movement, did not surprise him. He knew it would happen sooner rather than later, and the Fathers knew it too, for the warning signs were obvious, mounting over the years of thralldom — it was the point, which all oppressors through the existence of humanity eventually faced, when no amount of repression could quash the people's desire for freedom and basic rights. That night was the first breath of hope for the oppressed, for armed oppression was the unmistakable sign of the beginning of the end to suffering. That night no amount of threats and repression could prevent the suffering people from expressing their collective sorrow, from taking to the streets...

He watched with terror as the beast was about to take the expected last bite of the prey it had been tormenting for a long time. He was terrified but not surprised, knowing the day would come. The main gate to the campus blew up, and through the dark smoke he saw a uniformed man with an RPG on his shoulder, the launcher still smoking. Before the smoke thinned the assaulters had stormed the building, five, ten, twenty, more still. They wore uniforms with no marks of distinction, and no identifying insignia. They were moving in an orderly fashion, soldiers used to urban assault, soldiers well trained, soldiers following orders.

The first bullets whizzed by his head. He ducked behind the nearest display case showing the photographs and letters of some of the prominent Jesuits, written on the occasion of the founding of the alma mater. The soldiers were gaining on him, one by one, guns at the ready, cold determination on their faces. It was no time to hide. He had to warn the others. It was the only way to redeem himself after he had failed to warn and save the patients who were under his care at the infirmary. He had failed them then, he could not fail the Fathers.

He ran to the quarters where the Fathers slept. On the way he saw the woman, the housekeeper, and her fifteen year old daughter, the look in their eyes that of expectancy of the tragedy.

He cried, 'They have come for you! Get out! Save yourselves!'

They did not reply, they did not see him.

The older woman shouted at the intruders as she made the sign of the cross, 'There is no redemption for a catholic who lays a hand on another! Leave now and save your souls! If you harm these Holy men you will burn in hell, as God is the witness!'

A bullet stopped her from delivering further curses. Another ended the daughter's life. The assaulters tramped on their bodies as they rushed in for the main target of their hunt.

The Fathers were not asleep. They felt the black veil descending upon the campus, step by step its cold breath embracing them in its final inhale. They heard the gunshots thundering over the city. They heard the campus gate blow up. They could have escaped, there was still time, but they decided not to run, not to hide. They faced their destiny for which they had prepared all those years, day after day of

death-threats, fuelled in their strength and determination by
the love of the people whom they served. They were dragged
out of their quarters, and he could feel their hearts beat as
they brushed by him. They went past him without taking
note. Why were they not fighting? Why were they not crying
for help, or mercy? They did not resist, for one did not fight
the inevitable. Their faces were peaceful, each emanating a
source of love and hope, ready to forgive, ready to give their
lives, knowing it was the only way to force the change, which
was not yet unattained by decades of peaceful protests,
prayers, activism and working from the ground up to make
the world a better place.

No, it cannot end this way! He can save them, he must!

He cried, ' They have come for you! Run! Save
yourselves!'

They did not hear him. They did not run. They let their
captors drag them out. They were thrown to their knees, the
killers with brutal satisfaction shouting at them to say their
last prayers. They did not. They had said them already. They
said them every night.

Then the guns were raised.

He screamed and ran to help, but the harder he ran the
greater became the distance between them.

'No!' he screamed as the guns were leveled at their heads.

His voice was drowned in ear-piercing noise.

32. The Mortal Coil

"No!"

Dorn woke up, perspiring profusely, his heart pounding, his chest rising in desperate gasps. For a long time he could not tell where he was. He could see nothing, as though a dark veil covered his eyes. Soon the first realization came to him. He was in the dingy hotel room, on the uncomfortable bed, a sheet over his head. He isolated the sound, persistent, whizzing. It was his mobile phone. His heart rose to his throat. A call could not mean good news, for they agreed not to communicate using devices this susceptible to surveillance.

"Yes!" he picked up his handset with urgency.

He recognized the voice before his mind comprehended the words. It was not the voice of Brother Anselm.

"Where are you?" Kachem shouted.

Not comprehending Dorn glanced at the time displayed on the screen of his mobile phone. 03:14.

"Dorn, you there?"

"Yes, I was just—"

"You were asleep. Sure, but not in your own room."

The last words acted as a bucket of cold water on his head. Dorn regained all his senses. Somewhere in Kachem's arrogance he detected irony. He could actually see the grin on the Major's face. What precipitated such a reaction?

"Got lucky, did you? He-he—"

The giggle explained what was on Kachem's mind, and Dorn breathed in with relief. The Major was not accusing him, and no death squad was at the door.

In an instant Kachem's voice changed, it could not be mistaken for anything but conceit.

"We've got him, Dorn! We've got him!"

"Him?" Dorn repeated,

"Him, Dorn! Him! You get over here on the double—"

The world spun in front of his eyes. Not possible! Not possible! How could Kachem have done it in so short a time? The answer came to him nearly as quickly as the question was formed. Kachem arrived in town armed with the knowledge of the whereabouts of his prey. But Dorn was here, safe and sound. Whom, then, did he the Major capture?

Dorn slipped out of the hotel through the main gate, and rushed to the location given him by Kachem. He could not find a taxi at this hour in the city on the brink of another civil war. The twenty minutes it took him to get there on foot were the most agonizing. Was it too late to save the one who deserved to never end up in the hands of these butchers? He prayed that Kachem's self-satisfied announcement was the result of a mistake, but the longer he walked the grimmer seemed the outcome, and the more desperate he became. In his desperation he planned to give himself up for exchange of the one more worthy to live on, but whatever plans his crazed mind plotted had shattered the moment he saw the familiar figure.

Maj. Kachem was loitering nervously outside a large wall of a property, which spanned the entire city block. It was an industrial zone peppered with sweatshops, but the Major's upset was not caused by the condition of the workers made to slave here.

"Goddamn-it!" Kachem cried out at Dorn's appearance out of the darkness, his countenance a combination of helplessness and desperation. He was visibly shaken, disturbed by events beyond his control. He cursed in the foulest language until it brought relief.

"They snatched him, and won't release!" Kachem cried, and continued with the foulest ethnic slurs.

"Who?" Dorn asked. Instead of an answer he sensed movement behind his back.

Two uniformed men leveled their assault rifles at Dorn.

He did not panic. He was beyond panic, his mind, tired from the extended anxiety, was alert enough to suppress the emotion. He considered his chances. It was one of those situations were immediate action was due, something any field operative would have engaged in instinctively. But Dorn was not a field agent. His hand reached to the small of his back too slowly to alert the soldiers. Before his fingers grasped the handle of the knife, Maj. Kachem spoke to the armed men.

"Everything's fine. He's my friend."

The barrels were lowered, but the soldiers remained in place, and Dorn felt their attention centered on him.

Kachem pulled on his arm, and the two withdrew several steps.

Dorn felt the officer's trembling fingers, and found the source of it in the loss of control of the situation. Moments later he found out what the situation entailed.

"They won't even let me see him!" Kachem ground his teeth when they were outside of the soldiers' hearing range.

"Who?" Dorn asked naïvely.

"We got wind at home. Our sources close to the expat groups alerted us about the Junta zeroing in on our man. I flew down to stop them, but I was too late. They snatched him!"

Kachem was furious, his anger directed as much at the locals as his own helplessness, at his inability to deal with a vassal whose actions contradicted orders issued thousands of miles up north.

"What happened?" Dorn asked, his heart at his throat.

"What happened?! They won't let me talk to him—"

"I still don't understand—"

"What's there to understand! We prop up their government, we finance their military, train their officers, and they spit in our faces. That's what happened!"

"Have you mobilized the embassy to exert pressure?" Dorn asked with sudden hope. Perhaps not all was lost? Perhaps he could still changed the fate of the one who deserved to live.

"The embassy?" Kachem snorted.

"Face it, Will!" Dorn cried, purposely dropping the rank, as the mission stipulated, and thus asserting equal position. "We blew it! It is time to pull diplomatic strings." He hoped involving the embassy would trigger diplomatic response and save a life.

"Not this time. Not when the Church is involved, and the possibility of a blowback runs high."

"Have we any other options?" Dorn cried in desperation.

"The undersecretary is working through intelligence channels. I'm waiting for the call."

The answer offered hope. Whatever the tactics of the spy agency, a captive stood better chances of surviving an interrogation from Kachem's hands, rather than these butchers'.

"When this is over, the dogs will be reminded who feeds them!" Kachem seemed to read in his mind.

"How did they find him?" Dorn asked in order to divert his own mind from helpless wandering.

"They intercepted a coded message sent from our secure terminal in the Building," Kachem said coldly, his every word a needle piercing Dorn's heart.

Kachem looked at him with suddenly sober eyes, but whatever might have gone though his head, he was not meant to ponder it.

The two wings of the large steel gate of the factory began to slide open. Dorn and Kachem were blinded by headlights of two vehicles leaving the property. They stepped aside as a black limousine passed by, followed by a military pick up. Instantly noticeable were the lack of plates on the limo, and the unmistakable bullet-proof steel of the vehicle. The car slowed down momentarily as it passed. The window would not slide open, but in the spar light penetrating from within they could make out three silhouettes. Dorn thought he recognized one of them — the huge burly figure bulging out of the uniform — the sensation the stronger for the person staring back at him. He did not have the mind to ponder the discovery, nor the time, for a uniformed officer followed the vehicles on foot, and waved the two Gringos in.

"He's all yours," the officer announced in flawless English. He turned on his heels and led them across the long courtyard.

Inside, old and rusty machinery filled most of the huge main hall. It smelled of machine oil, and industrial waste, though the state it was in suggested it was not used for its intended purpose for a long time. The officer led them through the darkness between the machines infallibly, and they soon found themselves crossing the hall and marching toward the only source of light — a faint glimmer seen from the far end of the hallway, so far that it appeared to disappear. As life escaping the mortal coil, Dorn thought and shivered.

As they neared, Dorn realized the light escaped through the crack in the open doors, where men moved inside the room. It was an office with cupboards stacked with folders, a copier, computers, and a multitude of office supplies that lined the walls. In the middle of the room stood a large desk. On top of it lay a man. His body was naked and badly mutilated. The two uniformed men present inside were hurriedly cleaning up, picking objects from the floor. One of the objects drew Dorn's attention as its metallic surface glistened in the light. It was a small plumber's torch. With that picture came the intense smell of burned flesh, and Dorn could not doubt what had transpired here. The world reeled before his eyes.

Lying on the table was Brother Anselm.

Dorn's friend and mentor had died a terrible death. A gag in his mouth was wrapped around his head, preventing not only screaming but also the use of the poison capsule. Burn marks on all delicate parts of the body, from the feet to the pelvis and the underarms, razor cuts on the chest, and pins driven underneath finger nails told of terrible suffering. Eerily, though, Brother Anselm's face was spared the physical torture. If the killers counted on the pleasure of watching pain they were met with disappointment. The expression on the face was that of bliss, and it was the more striking for the stark contrast with the tortured body.

"What in God's name—?" Kachem started when the first shock wore off. The circumstances and time taken to inflict such meticulous pain was evidence of something other than mere interrogation. An experienced an officer as he was, Maj. Kachem felt insulted. He turned to the officer who led them in and immediately vented his frustration in the foulest of insults.

Dorn was on the verge of succumbing to overwhelming sorrow. What kept his mind alert was the realization of a pressing need to warn the courier. Lacking the experience of his superior officer he did not recognize the torture as an act of personal grievance, and saw it as the beginning of an all-out assault on the Company. Too, Maj. Kachem's fury did not allow him to withdraw into himself to grieve.

Kachem's anger blinded him to Dorn's emotional state. Had he been able to constrain his rage he would have noticed the glistening eyes, which Dorn could not conceal.

Having insulted the uniformed man, Kachem returned to his subordinate.

"Those sons-of-bitches! They killed him! They killed our best hope at finding the quickest possible route to the courier and the mole, for this man was the closest link to both!"

"Why would they do this?" Dorn asked through his trembling lips.

"Old grievances never die," Kachem replied sententiously.

Old grievances! It explained the bulletproof limo, an unmistakable sign of a Junta notable. The same Junta responsible for the attack on the Universidad, and the killing of the six Jesuits, carnage witnessed by one who survived, and who spread the truth about what initially was blamed on the rebels. Brother Anselm was marked for death ever since that fateful November night, more than two decades ago, yet he returned to the country regularly, if incognito. He came back to the rural communities the Jesuits cared for, delivering the much needed and often basic supplies, which made the difference between life and death to the poor, but jeopardized his own. Every such trip was marked, but never overshadowed, by real and present danger posed by the killers who sought to finish off the operation planed with surgical precision, the operation to remove the Company from the country. Twenty years ago the attack on the University backfired. Brother Anselm survived, and the world found out about the real killers. The martyrdom of the six Jesuits made the Company the stronger, but the blowback resulted from the botched assassination made the Junta the more determined to continue on the murderous path, a path of no return. Now, it seemed, they finally caught up with the one who cheated fate.

"He was the splinter in the eye of the Junta." Kachem seemed to read in Dorn's mind. "We have to act fast, Dorn, before the news reaches the courier."

"How can it?"

"Don't doubt for a minute that it was done so as to send a message to the rest of the Company."

Kachem took out his mobile phone, and scrolled through his contact list.

"How did they catch him?" Dorn asked.

Kachem raised a hand.

"Hold on," he said. Then he spoke to the handset, "Hollie— Get over here on the double—"

Suddenly Dorn understood. Blood rushed into his face. He stood frozen, his mind rushing.

"You were saying?" Kachem slipped the phone into his pocket.

Dorn did not reply, overwhelmed by a sudden desire to inflict punishment. Brother Anselm falling into the hands of the butchers could not have been a coincidence. He eluded the death squads for years, crossing the border regularly. He has done it countless times, traveling under an assumed name, and never raising the attention of the military and its death squads, until the day his likeness fell on the laps of Maj. Hollie Weader. Dorn understood now why the woman said nothing to him or to Kachem about the man she saw in Dorn's company. With his jaws and fists clenched, Dorn struggled to regain control, to quash the burning desire to tear the woman apart with his bare hands.

"The courier is our immediate concern," Kachem pressed. "I spoke with Hollie. We'll convene in half an hour. Before we do we ought to find out if they got anything out of this man."

Dorn recognized an ominous tone in Kachem's voice, and followed numbly.

They looked for the officer, undisturbed by the soldiers who moved about the property moving unidentified items into their vehicles. They found him outside the gate. Smoking a cigarette, he appeared to have the situation under control, awaiting for his soldiers to carry out whatever orders they were given. Pacing back and forth, he stopped when the two approached, and extended his arm with a pack of cigarettes in his hand.

Kachem struggled to contain his fury.

"You just fucked up one hell of an important operation," he hissed through his teeth.

The officer lit a cigarette and inhaled deeply.

"Need I remind you are not on your turf?" he said without raising his voice.

Dorn thought the soldier's hand trembled when he took several puffs. He looked closer and recognized intelligence corps insignia on the collar.

"Officer," he started quickly, in an effort to mitigate the standoff, aware that this man, who might have personally tortured his friend, might offer the best chance at advancing the mission. Checking himself against the desire to punish, he put on a face, and said, "Our countries are allies in the struggle against common enemy. We were close to delivering a major blow to the Company. With the killing of this man we lost the advantage."

Dorn was banking on the universal brotherhood of spies, on the understanding that intelligence officers might serve different countries — friendly, or at war — but regardless of ideology, or political objectives, their operations exists beyond the boundaries, geographical, religious, or ideological. Being the ones who risked their necks in the field, the ones ultimately responsible for successes or failures of their covert missions, they often relied on their own sense of understanding of geopolitical necessities. Dorn hoped the officer would grasp and appreciate his diplomatic approach.

The soldier appeared to share his foreign counterpart's concerns.

"Political motivations don't always go hand in hand with the strategic ones," he said.

"Which explains why military intelligence ought not take orders from civilians," Dorn appeased. "What happened there might well have stalled an important operation, but perhaps not ruined it. Not, if we act quickly."

"Are we allies?" the officer asked through a cloud of smoke.

"We're the closest allies in the region."

"Allies share intelligence."

"That they do."

"And enemies.

Dorn nodded.

"Then we both know the man was a priest with the Company."

"But only one of us knows what he divulged under— the interrogation."

"If there was an interrogation."

Dorn froze. He was right. What happened to Brother Anselm was personal.

"Then he did not talk?"

"Oh, he talked, but only what he wanted to say."

"What did he say, for God's sake?" Kachem exploded.

"*Ad maiorem Dei gloriam*. For the greater glory of God."

Dorn gasped, and turned his face to hide uncontrollable tears.

Both men looked at him, puzzled.

33. Standoff

Dorn's mind was ablaze. He struggled to keep himself in check. His suspicions were confirmed. Brother Anselm's torture and killing were long time in coming, and Dorn could not help but blame himself. He should have given in to his carnal instincts and kill the beast of the Sierra Madres when he had the opportunity. Now the killer struck again and murdered the dearest person of all. Who had facilitated the murder? Who sold out Brother Anselm to the butchers? Who will do the same to the courier?

Dorn clenched his teeth to prevent himself from shouting. He remained thus for the duration of the car ride, until Kachem pulled over his rental to the curb in Colonia Rosa, an affluent residential neighborhood of foreign diplomatic missions and wealthy industrialists.

Capt. Hollie Weader was waiting at an agreed upon location — a tiny park of decorative shrubs grown around a murmuring fountain. She avoided eye contact with the sort of forced determination often associated with guilt. Did she

161

not know what fate awaited the man she sold out to the torturers?

"Are you two going to stand here all sore?" Kachem's voice cut through the still air like a machete. He sensed the tension, but misconstrued its source. "Sometimes we win, sometimes we lose. It's the nature of the job. Let's roll up our sleeves and get on with the operation before it's too late."

Dorn said nothing, his eyes searching for minute expressions on the woman's face. His legs spread slightly to allow easy maneuvering, his right arm along his thigh, ready to draw out the knife from the small of his back, he waited for the woman's move.

She reached into her handbag.

This was no time to talk, to argue, or to ask questions. Words were needless, anyway. They both knew it. The woman saw Dorn with the elder whose face was on the sketch. Then the man was tortured and killed.

In one swift move Dorn reached and grasped the handle of the knife, pulling it out, the blade glistening ominously in the light cast from the nearest lamppost. Before he struck, his eye registered the object the woman drew out of her handbag.

At the same instance Kachem spat out with the speed of a machine gun, "What the hell is wrong with you, Dorn!? Our situation has become more complicated, but the objective has not changed — the courier must leave this place unharmed!"

The split-second hesitation caused by the recognition of the object in the woman's hand, followed by Kachem's outburst, prevented a tragedy. Maj. Kachem was right. The courier was the priority. A time to settle scores shall come later.

The woman's lips trembled as her eyes watched the blade. She forced herself to look away, her eyes on the mobile phone she held in her hand.

"I received a message from my contact. I've been cleared to meet the courier."

"When?"

"Tomorrow."

Kachem cursed. The expletives appeared to bring relief. He gathered his thoughts, took several deep breaths, and said, "We've no choice but to use everything at our disposal to stall the locals who seem on the quest to ruin our op. I was blinded by thinking these dogs were obedient, but their settling their own scores with the Company proves they've gone astray. It's the same story in all these places where the security forces, though funded by us, remain in fact at the service of the narrow group of plutocrats who rule from behind their walled fortresses." He gazed into the closest wall and spat.

"What are we to do?" Capt. Weader asked, her voice timid, her eyes continuing to avoid Dorn's.

"The only thing one ought to do in these banana republics. In a place where a handful of families dictate the policy of an entire country one must squeeze them by their balls. I thought we did, but, apparently, not hard enough. They were told not to interfere with our operation, come what may, and they did the opposite. Now we'll have to make them understand who they owe their privileged position to."

Dorn nodded. It suited him to occupy the Major with something, anything, which took him off Dorn's back, now that every minute counted and pretenses had to be dropped in favor of expediency. He ought to have found words of encouragement to ensure Kachem did as he said, but Dorn could not, his mind wholly centered on the woman. Capt. Weader presented the more immediate danger, more so for her unknown motivations. Why did she give away Brother Anselm to the tortures? And why did she not inform Kachem about Dorn's contact with the slain priest?

"Come!" Kachem completed a call on his mobile phone, and started for the car.

The morning sun was rising over the buildings when the car pulled in at the plaza. They left the vehicle and took a table in front of a coffee shop, with a view of the hotel across the still sleepy square. They sat for a time without a word, each engrossed in their own thoughts, quietly sipping coffee. It seemed a precious moment of peace, but peace only superficial for each boiled under their skin.

Dorn's entire attention centered on his cup, he was thinking about the one who was responsible for his friend's death, and was sitting within an arm's reach. He attributed his remarkable self-restraint to the emotional and physical fatigue, coupled with the sense of duty to the Company. And so it happened that his heart was demanding one thing, but his mind held him back from unleashing vengeance on the one who was now his only conduit to the courier.

He observed the woman from the corner of his eye. She did not touch her drink, and sat straight, stiff, her eyes on some unspecified spot of the plaza. What went through her mind? What was the meaning of her silence? Was it part of the game to unsettle her prey? Did she require further proof of Dorn's guilt?

Dorn's train of thought was broken by the sudden appearance of two large men. One resembled a pit bull, and the other a rottweiler. They towered over the coffee table and its battered occupants.

"Maj. Kachem!" said the one who resembled a pit bull, his words spoken with a strong southern drawl.

"Goddamn!" Kachem cursed, startled. "What are you doing here?"

Apparently they had met before, Dorn thought. Kachem's reaction told him the Major had been busy since his arrival in town.

"I have orders to assist you, Sir."

A military man, Dorn recognized from the way the words were spoken.

"What the hell you drawling about?" Kachem was nonplussed.

In reply the man glanced tellingly to the Major's companions.

"Just say what it is you want!" Kachem barked.

"The ambassador wants to see you, Sir."

"What in the hell for?" Kachem asked, his voice devoid of surprise.

What, indeed, Dorn thought. What connects the Major and the ambassador, and why the hostility? He glanced at his superior officer, and through him to the woman, whose pale face and eyes anchored firmly on the concrete pavement suggested she was as disconcerted about the affair as the rest of them.

"Did I not make myself abundantly clear that I mustn't be associated with the embassy?" Kachem followed his last question with another, delivered in a sterner tone.

"Unfortunately, the embassy is very much involved now, Sir. You and the ambassador have both been summoned to the foreign ministry to explain the nature of your presence in the country."

Maj. Kachem nearly choked on the coffee.

Dorn caught the woman's eyes as they glided to the strangers. Minute muscle contractions on her face told him she understood the implication of the summons correctly. The Junta called on the embassy for explanation about the operation. The ambassador, not informed, as was customary in cases of black ops, had found himself in an embarrassing position having to make the best of a bad job.

Dorn realized it was likely a continuation of the events of the night, of the Junta's determined drive locate of the courier, and he could not help but smile internally. He found himself in a situation from which he could benefit. Any animosity, which tied the hands of his opponents gave him an advantage. With the Junta and its death squads at odds with Kachem and the ambassador, Dorn had only Weader to contend with, for he could not doubt the Major would pull out big guns to respond to the insult.

Dorn was not mistaken.

His face as grey as the pavement in front of the coffee shop, Maj. Kachem hissed, "Tell the ambassador to tell the minister that I am not here, never was!"

"I'm afraid you will have to tell him that yourself, Sir." The reply came with a warning, the pit bull's eyes gliding over to the rottweiler.

"Those sons-of-bitches!" Kachem exploded. "They know what they're doing, but what sons-of-bitches!" He let his steam off, and demanded several moments of privacy.

The two embassy men withdrew.

"Now, you listen up, both of you," Kachem turned to his companions. "We have much less time. It's obvious the locals want to upset our plans. Why? I don't know, but I'll get to the bottom of it, and heads will roll. Meanwhile, I want you to carry on. I authorize you to use any means necessary to complete your mission." He turned to the woman, "Do not wait till tomorrow. Find the courier today and, above all, whatever happens, ensure the courier leaves this place alive."

"What if they beat us to him?" Dorn asked not without concern.

"There will be no more obstructions," Kachem spat out with savory hatred in his eyes. "The horseshit's just hit the fan, and these dogs will be reminded of the chain of command in this godforsaken place."

Then he was gone.

They sat without a word for some time. Dorn sensed the woman relaxed somewhat after Kachem's departure. He understood it, for he too relaxed without Kachem's radiating tension pinching his every nerve. On the other hand the electric tension between the two was no longer diffused by Kachem's presence. Sparks flew between them. Anything could ignite and cause an explosion, something Dorn wanted to avoid, his mission requiring complete submission of emotions.

The volcano brewing in his heart was hard to contain, the eruption inevitable. In order to suppress it, but keenly aware of the need to keep the woman within his sight, he said in a hoarse voice, "Join me for breakfast?"

She did not look at him, her eyes on her shoes.

"Risk being crucified by Kachem? No, better get on with the job."

Why the lassitude, Dorn wondered. He gawked at her inconspicuously. Did he recognize beads of sweat or were those tears under her eyes? He decided on the latter, and was puzzled. Could she have been tormented by guilt? It would show a frail human being behind the beastly deed.

Dorn was suddenly struck with a perverse question. What would Brother Anselm do in his position? Would he find the compassion to forgive? Dorn did not like the answer forming in his mind. He was not Brother Anselm, he was not ordained, but instead whisked away from priesthood to put on a different uniform. This ought to have absolved him from the forgive-and-forget mantra of his brothers who would undoubtedly have advocated it. Yet, he could not help but admit they were right. To build a better world one ought to surrender the old ways of settling scores, and use actions becoming of a new, better world. How could he, though? How could he forget what this woman had done? How could he forgive when the memory of her act was etched in his mind forever? Overwhelmed by the troubling thoughts, he could not speak.

The silence became electric.

He watched the woman stand up. He watched as she began to walk away. He wanted to follow, to clasp her arm, to pull her hair, and to shout: Enough! You have done enough damage! No more!

He stood up, the chair falling onto the ground behind him, its legs somehow twisted between Dorn's. The momentary obstacle drew his attention to its source. He freed himself and rushed after her when he was met with a familiar voice.

"Out for a morning stroll?" asked Foras Helborn.

34. In Pursuit

Several paces to his right, Foras Helborn was sitting in a high chair, a local newspaper on his lap, a short man of indeterminate age was shining his shoes with bare hands. Helborn's eyes gleamed with sarcasm and something else, which Dorn could not discern. Had the vile man observed what transpired?

"These mornings are something else, don't you think?" Helborn asked.

Fatigued by the events of the night and incensed by the least expected sight of the despicable face, Dorn replied in a less diplomatic manner than he would have in other circumstances. His biting reply would come back to haunt him, and would bring him within an ace of death.

"The ghostly convents lose their eeriness in this light, I'm sure."

The shot went home. The newspaper trembled in Helborn's hands, his face turned pale, his pupils narrowed, and he resembled a night beast caught by daylight.

He forced a belated smile, and said, "Why, yes, and if I may advise, you've come to the right place. This country is rich in unrivalled religious architecture."

"I've heard of a place where skeletons of an old convent hide the eerie secrets of people who appear among its walls, disoriented, incomplete—"

Helborn crumpled the newspaper and jumped to his feet. He threw two coins to the shoeshine and walked away briskly, never turning his head.

Dorn watched him with a faint gleam of satisfaction. He felt lighter, the exchange, though short, had released his steam. Brother Anselm's information was on the money. Dorn could not mistake Helborn's reaction for anything but admission to the charges laid by Juan, the church keeper. What could he do with the secret? As his eyes followed the quickly disappearing figure his mind filled with growing contempt and determination. People such as Helborn ought to pay for their inhuman craft. They ought to pay for the pain they cause. How? Dorn did not know, but of one thing he was certain — the outing of Helborn's past would cause a reaction. Manipulating people, causing reactions, and acting upon them, was a crucial part of Dorn's work. He did it, he roused the hated beast of a man, and all he had to do now was summon up his patience, and wait.

Occupied by the confrontation, however short lived, Dorn lost sight of Capt. Weader. He started in the direction she walked off, and quickened pace, but to no avail. She was gone, on the quest to destroy the Company. Breathless, faced with no other alternative, he continued across the plaza, and onto the street connecting it with the Mercado. The sun shone into his eyes, blinding him. He crossed the street to the shaded side, and his peripheral vision caught familiar colors and shape. His heart jumpstarted. Capt. Weader stood by the entrance to a bakery, a small paper bag in her hand, mobile phone in the other. Dorn could not hear the words, but judging by the woman's body language and gesticulation of the hand, which held the bag of pastries, the conversation was dramatic, and responsible for drawing his attention. He thanked the providence, and sunk into a wall recess, waiting.

Weader started within moments, and crossed the street onto the sunny side. He followed her, taking cover behind the parked cars. To his chagrin the woman hailed an approaching taxi. Dorn cursed. He could not lose her, not now, when something in the purposeful way in which she moved told him Capt. Weader was onto something. Suddenly he remembered and reached into his pocket. He found it. Not all was lost.

The one way street with the traffic moving toward him offered him a window of opportunity. He sprinted back. As Brother Anselm had promised a yellow moped was chained to a post behind the hotel. He unlocked it, and started the engine in time to see the taxi disappear around the corner of the plaza.

Keeping a safe distance, Dorn maneuvered the moped amid pick ups topped with workers and various material, minivans used as buses, and still more taxis. He was reasonably certain the woman would not spot the pursuit, but should she make him out in the busy morning traffic he was determined to pursue it to the end, whatever it might bring.

Soon the taxi joined a major street where it became a challenge to avoid being clipped by passing vehicles, most of which were headed to the Mercado, the drivers engaged in all manners of illegal maneuvers. The taxi slowed along with the flow and Dorn's heart began to race. He cursed whoever picked it as a point of the rendezvous, for the elbow-to-elbow crowds of the market, and multiple exits, made it an ideal place to blend-in and disappear.

To his relief, the woman's meeting place was not the Mercado.

The taxi drove on, and soon it joined a big thoroughfare where commanding a moped among dilapidated tractor-trailers became a harrowing experience, tantamount to flying a two-seater next to a jumbo jet. Having to drive close to the curb, his nerves strained to the limits, Dorn was grateful he did not lose the taxi, vanishing though it was. He caught up with it only by the University campus, which fed countless vehicles to the freeway, causing traffic to slow down. He looked at the buildings where he spent his formative year, and where the six Jesuits were murdered by the Junta, and his heart refueled with determination. The University, this symbol synonymous with the Company, stood proud, imposing, seemingly impervious.

Some minutes later the taxi passed the municipality of Santa Tecla, where it took an exit and began to climb a steep serpent road onto a volcanic mountain with wooded slopes. They began to climb. Several hairpin curves made Dorn's heart drum with terror as the moped's wheels spun on dirt, dangerously close to the precipice beneath. He could not pullover to a nonexistent shoulder, the steady nose-to-bumper traffic forcing him to keep pace despite the hair-rising ascent. To make things worse, vehicles began to pass him, drivers frustrated with the low-powered moped. Streaming sweat began to tickle his neck and chest, flooding his eyes. Afraid to release the steering bar, unable to wipe his eyes, he cursed and blew air through the corners of his mouth, to no avail. Soon he had lost sight of the taxi and continued on out of stubbornness and determination. He was losing the battle, though solely due to the shortcomings of his tiny two-wheeler, his long legs wrapped around it making many a driver honk and laugh. The image of himself drew a nervous laughter from his throat. Soon he laughed hysterically, and the moped began to sway, claiming more of the paved surface, preventing cars from passing, their drivers daring not follow too closely the *loco* who seemed oblivious to the dangers of the road nicknamed *el mirador de muerte* for its spectacular vistas, which drew too many inattentive motorists to plunge into the void beneath.

Had Dorn not been in a state of near emotional breakdown he might have noticed and recognized one particular vehicle, which followed him from the city, its presence becoming clear on the serpent road as it was the only vehicle, which did not pass him, matching his slow pace throughout.

At last the road neared its highest elevation, and continued on along a flattened ridge. Dorn turned up the gas, but his hopes of catching up with the taxi began to wane even as his speed increased. Several taxis were visible ahead, each putting on a distance now that the road was slightly wider, no longer climbing. His hope was almost gone when spotted a dust cloud on the side of the road.

In the distance, obscured by shrubbery, stood a lone figure. As Dorn neared, the dust began to set, and he could swear the figure was that of the woman he was pursuing. She disappeared into the brush, and below the grade of the road. By the time he arrived at the site she was gone.

The shoulder here was wide enough for a vehicle to pull over, and Dorn hid the moped behind a large boulder, only steps away from a clearing in the thorn brush. He began to descend on foot, and soon found a dry rain run off bed. He continued on at breakneck speed, risking injury, but it paid off. He spotted the woman at a distance, below, just in time before she took a turn at the fork. It was, indeed, Capt. Hollie Weader.

The heat was excruciating despite the early hour, the sun pounding down mercilessly. Dorn was thirsty, and felt dirt clinging to his sweaty face and all exposed body parts, but the renewed hope kept all discomfort in check. Now that he found the woman he continued the steep descent with caution, conscious of alerting her, and in the process scraping his arms and tearing his pants on thorns. Soon the engine roar of the road waned and ended, the silence broken only by the footsteps and heavy breathing. Dorn slowed and added distance between them so as not to alert the woman to the stones rolling from underneath his feet. Every now and then she disappeared behind a bend, and he stepped up speed. At one point, just as he wiped his face with a sleeve of his shirt, he found her standing in place, and he had a strange feeling she was waiting for him, but concluded she was merely surveying yet another fork in the path, and picked one just as Dorn emerged from around the bend.

He followed her for a quarter of an hour. Several times the woman vanished behind curves in the terrain, but was never too far when he caught up, and he wondered if the excursion was a ruse to lead him into a trap. Whatever her intentions he could not back down. He learned to anticipate her moves, staying close, but within an easy duck into the bushes or behind boulders. He found comfort in the realization of how difficult she would find it to spot him, with the sun shining directly from behind his back.

At last the woman reached what seemed the destination — a clearing between the thorn shrubbery and a small valley with green pastures, and a pond surrounded by orange groves.

35. Remorse

Earlier, as she crossed the plaza, Hollie's mind was a basket of worries. What happened at night was a natural outcome of the stupidity of men. She blamed Kachem. His arrival in town had distracted her, and led to the capture and torture of the old man, something she would never have allowed had she been in a position to stop it. It was a useless and senseless death. Coercion and torture did not apply to the members of the Company. The Jesuits would sooner die a painful death than talk. The only thing the capture and the brutal killing accomplished was to send the rest of them for cover. Kachem gained nothing. His arch enemy was killed, but the Company would only emerge the stronger for it, unified, more determined. And Dorn? What was his part in it? Why taunt her with his ostentatious meetings with the Brother? Was he baiting her? Was she a suspect in the notorious Major's quest to smoke out uncertain elements from the force? Did the CIFA have a reason to suspect her? All things considered she fit the profile: she worked with religious orders, and she often returned to the Building. Was it enough to mark her as the mole they were after? Everything suggested they needed the final proof, hence Dorn's fraternizing with the Brother, and Kachem's giving up the old man for torture. The CIFA ruined many an officer's career simply by casting suspicions, but they were wrong thinking they could break her. She was strong, determined, and above all smarter than the rest of them put together. She would show them yet.

Despite her bravado, Hollie was painfully aware that whether their suspicions were founded or not, once Kachem set his ugly eyes on someone the person was finished professionally. They did not trust her, and this was the material fact. The fools! That Kachem was guided by a single-track mind did not surprise her, but she thought better of Dorn, and she admitted it to herself without undue prudence. The two days they spent together were enough to form desire for this handsome, philosophical man. Of course, she knew he was setting a trap for her from the moment she saw him with the elderly man on the airplane. She thought she could convince Dorn of her faithful service, and tried again and again, each time running into an impenetrable barrier. She knew she had lost when he darn near accused her of killing Fink. Strangely, she remained attracted to him. He was incorruptible, devoted to what he believed in. She admired it in a man and could not imagine her feelings for him would remain the same had he dropped his suspicions on account of a few drinks and her misty eyes. The worst kind of spy was one who gave up his ideals, who betrayed his values, for he was a candidate to change them again, and again.

She sighed and shook her head. What a waste, that a man like Dorn must be removed from her way.

That morning, on the plaza, she parted with Dorn, and made certain she would remain within visible range. She waited as he chatted with a man who was having his shoes shined. She recognized the obnoxious drunkard from the airplane, and was not surprised, pegging him as yet another of Kachem's agents out to ensnarl her. So they worked together. So much the better. She would teach all three of them a lesson. She watched Dorn and this man, what did he call himself? Helborn? She watched them exchange several words, saw them part, all animated, as though their minds were made up about her. Whatever was decided between them, it was Dorn who followed her, as she hoped he would. She watched him approach with spring in his step, and she could not help but recall that night of dance and wine. She still felt his nimble arms around her waist, she felt his breath on her neck. She watched him approach now, though he could not yet see her, blinded by the early sun. She saw him as clear as day, in his eyes fierce determination. In those eyes was the final confirmation. She was his target. She could no longer doubt it. She made a quick telephone call, and her contact arranged to send in one of his men, a taxi driver.

She entered the cab, and her heart rushed when she saw Dorn turn on his heels. He did not hail another taxi to follow her. Run, save yourself! she thought. He did not. As her cab passed the hotel she saw him start a small moped and follow. She sighed. It was the most ill-chosen vehicle for the pursuit. Bright yellow, shiny, new, it stood out among the beaten old cars. Of course, she reminded herself, conspicuous surveillance was not Kachem's tactic, and she could expect no less from the Major's disciple. How could they hope to succeed in their battle against the Company? They were brutes, simpletons who thought they could fight an idea. Poor Dorn. Too late to convert you, my handsome adversary. If only you weren't so darn suspicious.

Her thoughts were no longer laced with remorse. Removing the overzealous man who was an obstacle to a successful completion of her own mission, was her priority. She shook her head, as though to clear her mind of the feelings she had for the man. Determined to follow through with the only solution at her disposal, she directed the driver not to lose the moped, but even so there were times when the small vehicle could not keep up. Dorn's determination allowed him to stay within visible range against all odds. It was not until they started the ascent to the volcanic mountain when she thought the moped stalled. She thought, perversely, though not without her heart drumming, that providence spared her the necessity to commit the grave sin.

Some of the hairpin curves were deadly dangerous. On several occasions, as they negotiated the extremely narrow curves, a deep void between them, she saw Dorn struggle to remain on the road, vehicles passing him, honking, pushing to within an inch of the precipice. It seemed a gust of wind could finish the job. Yet, he prowled on, though the distance between them grew. The taxi could not hold the traffic, and at last, when she was dropped off, she thought he would not make it. He did. She saw him approach, driving in the hot glaze of the sunrays bouncing of the asphalt. He was coming to meet his fate.

36. Trapped

Dorn hesitated before crossing the clearing, for the first time seeing clearly that it would expose him, and turn him into an easy target for whoever might be lurking in the grove on the other side of the barren strip. He watched the woman descend to the luscious valley in a light gait, too light, as though a heavy ballast was lifted off her shoulders, and he wondered whether he was the ballast she was shedding. His mind replayed the events, which led him to pursue the woman, and found nothing to suggest she had led him into a trap. He could not retreat, anyway, for this, in his mind, was his only opportunity to reach the courier.

Dorn entered the clearing and followed in the woman's steps. He did not reach the other side when he was stopped by a gruff voice of a person he could not see, and who commanded him in Spanish.

"Stay where you are."

It took him a split second to calculate his odds. He was exposed, in plain view, without the benefit of seeing his adversary. He dared not disregard the warning, lest he die ridden with bullets. He stood motionless. Momentarily two men emerged from the grove, automatic weapons in their hands.

"Watch out, he may be armed!" a woman's voice warned.

Capt. Hollie Weader appeared from the thicket, an expression of pained satisfaction on her face.

Dorn was not frightened, instead feeling of disappointment showed on his face. He did not resist. No one would when faced with loaded rifles aimed at his abdomen. But he did not resist for yet a more important reason. Here was a clear opportunity to reach the courier, and reach him he would, whether arrested or otherwise.

He followed the lead man with relief, which was brought about by the nearing culmination of the tremendous effort that meant so much to so many. He walked lightly, despite exhaustion, driven by anticipation, convinced every step brought him closer to the courier. The realization it would not happen took him by surprise, and stripped him of the ability to react, to change the inevitable outcome, when the barrels of the guards' rifles directed him toward what resembled the stables, whereas the woman continued on, toward a house that appeared some hundred steps down the green pasture.

The location was not as desolate as it appeared at first. He observed as Hollie approached the edifice, a bungalow with solar panels on the roof. For the next minute or two he had hoped she would emerge with the courtier, but minutes passed and nothing happened. Resigned, he reassessed his situation. He could not cross the stretch of grass that separated the stables from the house, without a bullet in the back. He could not reason with the guards. He would not try to do so, either, for they seemed the type who would follow orders blindly. They were well chosen for their task, and Dorn could not fault them. Too, he reasoned, he ought not break his cover in front of them, for when the episode was over he would return to his duties, and the fewer knew what these entailed the more valuable the intelligence he could continue to provide.

He listened to the guards exchange several words in colloquial Spanish, and surmised they would take no action without orders from someone in charge. Thus he sat down on a wooden crate, next to a heap of hay, and waited, his eyes on the house.

Their captive's lack of fear and irreverence for the command structure infuriated the guards. Dorn sensed their pent up anticipation, and smiled in his mind at the coming surprise. But as time passed, his condition unchanged, Dorn began to worry. Soon he became stricken with doubt. The woman fooled the courier, and passed herself off as agent of the Company. Her identity had been carefully crafted to fit into the place of the woman she was impersonating. Her word, the word of a valuable asset whom she impersonated, one who delivered far and beyond the expectations placed on her, was a strong card. Worse still: It occurred to him possible her ingenuity could peg him as the Company's worst enemy. Naturally he could prove his bona fides, but what if he was not given the chance? What if he never met with the courier? The thought cause all hair to stand up high on his head. He was not concerned for his safety, for despite his young age he was prepared to lay the ultimate sacrifice when circumstances called for it. This, however, was neither the time, nor the place. He could not perish at the hands of his comrades. He could not wait passively while the woman wrecked further damage.

No, he could not wait idly any more!

"I must see the courier!" Dorn demanded in English.

He knew they understood him when they commented among themselves, but did not accommodate his demand.

Dorn stood up abruptly and repeated his words.

One of the men, who appeared in charge of the two-person team, approached him, and, without a warning, delivered a blow to his solar plexus.

Dorn fell onto the hay. Struggling to regain his breath he writhed when his peripheral vision registered movement outside the house.

The woman walked out onto the green lawn, followed by a man. From the distance Dorn determined the man was his late sixties. His clerical provenance was unmistakable even through the civilian clothes he wore. His gait was that of a self-assured high-ranking member of society, or a professed Father of high-standing within the Company, one used to receiving reverence equal only to that of a true prince of the Church, though of infinitely higher regard, for the Jesuits considered bishopric or a Cardinal's hat beneath the true calling of a priest. Dorn could not doubt this was the courier, a man privy to some of the most sensitive affairs of the most powerful Catholic Order, a man close to the leadership of the Company and the Church, and finally a man who fell for the devious plotting of the worst enemy. The rapport between the two was the evidence of the woman's successful mission. With her hand under the courier's arm she appeared triumphant, speaking to him incessantly, undoubtedly poisoning his mind with lies. Both seemed oblivious to the existence of the prisoner.

It was time to end the charade.

Dorn struggled to a seated position, and took several deep breaths. Having changed his viewing angle, from a horizontal to a vertical, he realized the pair had no intention of coming to the stables. Worse still they approached a vehicle parked on the side of the house. He watched as the man opened the passenger door and the woman took her seat.

"No!" Dorn sprung to his feet.

Two barrels kept him in check. He dared not move lest the highly tense guards take a step of no return.

The commotion caught the attention of the courier. He addressed the woman, who turned her head to the stables.

For a brief moment her eyes locked with Dorn's. In those eyes he recognized that his fate had been sealed.

As though in confirmation one of the guards answered his mobile phone, the call initiated by the courier. The guard listened intently, his gaze shooting to the prisoner, avoiding his eyes.

This was not a good look, Dorn opined. His ears caught a reply given in Spanish.

"*Si, Padre … Comprendo.*"

The guard folded his phone, and turned to his companion, his eyes straining to avoid Dorn's. Having surmised that their prisoner understood no Spanish, he said, "We take him to the mountains."

Dorn understood what hid behind the statement. The mountains were a refuge, a safe haven for those members of the Company who could not hide anywhere else. Impassable, virgin jungle forests offered relative safety from death squads, and could just as well serve as internment camps for the Company's enemies, humanely removed from the world where their actions could endanger others. Many who were interned in such camps, who were given the chance to learn the ways of the Company, were rehabilitated, converted, became fervent proponents of the causes they once fought. Now, in the case of mistaken identity, and some devious conniving, Dorn's guards received orders to whisk him away into one such camp in the mountains. It was not the time to argue or plead. He knew it would not do. Having issued the order, the courier returned to the vehicle. To try to explain to the guards the mistake would have meant the loss of precious seconds. These men would not sway from their orders.

Dorn adjusted his feet in such a way as to allow himself a quick response. His muscles flexed, he awaited the right moment. It came when the leading guard slipped the mobile phone into his pocket, while simultaneously and inadvertently shifting the barrel of his automatic. Dorn chose that moment to spring to his feet, and lunged at the man, while the weapon continued its downward sway.

His body impact brought the man down, and landed both of them on the younger of the guards. All three fell onto the concrete floor, the younger guard's head grazing a thick metal bar of the box used to house the horses. This was not a chance to miss and Dorn was not a man to think twice in a situation of life and death. His elbow delivered a powerful blow to the jaw of the man whom he fell on top of, and was ready to repeat the procedure on the other, when he realized that both were rendered incapacitated.

It was over sooner than he could have hoped, but the struggle proved too strenuous having been undertaken shortly after the blow to the solar plexus. The humid air of the stables did not help either, and Dorn found himself lying on top of the pile of bodies, gasping for air. Bathed in perspiration he struggled to his feet, and towered on his swaying legs over the two guards. He could not help but wonder over their peaceful, lovers-like embrace.

37. Revenge

Dorn gave chase after the vehicle but it was no use. The courier and the woman were gone, and he feared the worst. Had it been Maj. Kachem who drove off with the courier, Dorn would not worry half as much. As it was, however, with the woman evidently pursuing her own agenda — one clearly different from the objective to allow the courier a safe return to the Company headquarters with the false information — Dorn could not help but fear for the courier's life. Having lost one already, a man close and dear to his heart, he could not allow the same to happen to another. Fixated on saving the life of the man he had never met, but whose service in the ranks of the Company was close to his own convictions, Dorn returned in search of a vehicle. Evidently, though, only one was used to serve the inhabitants of the remote dwelling. With no other option left to him he sprinted up the path, which had earlier brought him down to this place.

To his relief the road was not nearly as far as the descent suggested. He realized it seemed further and higher due to the woman's meandering in purposeful deception. And it was thus that he found himself on the side of the road and starting the engine of the small moped in under a quarter of an hour. It was not until this moment that Dorn was struck with the one important question — Where to?

With his mind occupied by worries and uncertainties, the drive down the narrow and curving road did not seem as petrifying as the ascent. Paying little attention to the precipice he turned up the gas and rolled down at the speed of a daredevil. The still and hot air did little to cool his body as the moped raced down the slopes of the volcano. Anxiety caused by the woman's deceit made him oblivious to the danger posed by the treacherous road as well as to the surroundings, his eyes and mind set firmly and only on the destination.

Had he been in his normal, alert state of mind, Dorn would have noticed a dusty sedan which was parked at the side of the road, squeezed into the slope, and which shot out when the moped passed it at high speed. He would have heard the horns of those vehicles which narrowly avoided collision with the sedan. He would have noticed the face of the driver who followed him. He would have become unbalanced at the sight of determination in the driver's eyes. He would have recognized a dogged desire to kill.

Foras Helborn's crazed face gleamed with pathological hatred as his sedan gained on the moped. He had followed Dorn from the city. He had watched him park the moped behind the thicket and a boulder. He had waited for Dorn to return, and he followed him with only one desire: No one who finds out what Dr. Helborn did for a living ought to remain alive!

Alas, the curving road did not allow him to exact quick and instant revenge. As much as Helborn wished death upon Dorn, he did not want to die himself. The brightly colored moped acted as a matador's rag on a bull, but Helborn's fury did not blind him entirely. He pressed on the breaks frequently so as not to lose control of the heavy vehicle. His sense of self-preservation was fueled by his want to see the demise of the hated man. He did not accept the possibility he might fail. Not now, not when he was this close. In his determination he bit his own lips, but felt no pain, taking pleasure in tasting the blood of his victim to be.

Unbeknownst to Helborn similar determination took over Dorn. Desperate to reach his destination he drove without regard for his safety, keeping a steady, and at times growing distance, between the moped and the sedan, causing Helborn to grow ever more anxious. As time went by, and the vehicles descended half way down the volcanic slope, the disgraced medic became desperate to feed his craving for blood. With the roofs of the Santa Tecla municipality taking shape below them, Helborn made the last effort to finish his deed. No longer able to judge external factors, such as the necessity to leave no witnesses, he floored the accelerator. The sedan's front bender struck the moped just as it neared a narrow curve.

Dorn did not realize what happened. The blow came out of the blue. He felt a powerful jolt and lost control of the steering bar. The moped lunged across the road and neared the edge of the cliff. The front wheel hit a protrusion in the road and the small vehicle tumbled, man and metal rolling, continuing on the path to their doom. Sparks flew as the metal scraped the asphalt, and were soon joined by a myriad of dust particles scraping off the narrow stretch of earth that preceded the precipice.

The moped shot out into the void.

In an impulse of survival Dorn grasped onto something, that seemed to fall into his open hand, his fingers closing in an iron grip, his eyes following the path of the flying vehicle. The short, but dense and strong brush that covered the slope saved him from following the machine. Hanging onto the thorny branches and earthy roots he watched the metal twist as it hit rocks, and tumble down until it became but a blotch of undetermined shape.

It was no time to ponder what happened. It was not necessary for the reason became clear when his eyes darted across the void and onto the road where a sedan slowed down, its driver's head focused on the mangled mass of metal below. The narrowly set, glowing eyes, and the red face of Foras Helborn explained everything.

With the car gone behind the bend, Dorn's legs felt the wall until his feet found support. Inch-by-inch he pulled himself up, and crawled out onto the miniscule side of the road. He lay there for some time, vehicles passing him inches away. Not one driver stopped to offer help to the bruised man. Doubtful whether anyone had noticed the event, which happened in the blink of an eye, on a narrow bend of a short stretch of the road, with drivers' attention centered on the fenders of the preceding vehicles.

Limping, Dorn descended on foot to the municipality of Santa Tecla where he found a taxi willing to pick up a disheveled passenger. Several hours had passed since the attack before he arrived at the hotel. He entered through the restaurant entrance and spent several agonizing seconds examining the door to his room. It appeared untouched, as requested by the Do Not Disturb sign, the single strand of hair remaining in its place at the lower part of the doorframe. Once inside he jumped into the shower and drank, and drank, before attending to his bruises. There were many. Water opened dry scabs and caused renewed bleeding, but he did not flinch. They were surface scratches. He treated all with what remained of the Mezcal the woman left two nights ago. He then downed the remnants of the alcohol, swallowing the traditional worm in whole.

Apart from the superficial wounds cleaned by soap and water, the alcohol took care of the internal, spreading its salutary effect to every cell of his body. Only now did it occur to him that he had nearly lost his life. If he had earlier hoped that confronting Helborn would bring a reaction, he now received it with usury. The despicable man did not want his secret out and was prepared to go to any length to protect it. The attempt on Dorn's life was proof of his dirty past. Helborn failed, but doubtless he would try something else when he found out Dorn had survived.

Dorn was compelled to find a way to do away with the medic who broke the Hippocratic Oath and caused pain and death to countless victims. For now, however, he had to attend to a more pressing matter.

He stepped out onto the balcony and looked down. People strolled leisurely below. It would not work this time, he could not reach the woman's room this way without raising attention to himself. He approached the dresser, and opened his carry on bag. He felt the seams and pulled out several metal wires, which he planned to use to jimmy the lock. Armed thus he rushed to the door.

His heart jumped when his hand reached the door handle...

38. The Plan

"Dorn!" Maj. Kachem walked in. "What the hell happened to you?" He looked his young colleague up and down.

"A road accident," Dorn uttered dismissively.

"Damn those drivers! They obey no rules. Not sure there are any. I too was nearly run over today. Twice!" Kachem swallowed the explanation without a flinch. In a rare bout of concern he added, "Seen a doc?"

Dorn studied his opposite's face for signs of a ruse. Whatever the origins and the nature of the relationship between Kachem and Helborn, as boasted by the latter, the murder attempt was not a joint venture. Though unbecoming, it was possible the Major was actually concerned for his officer, a discernible scent of alcohol making it the more plausible.

"I'm fine," he replied in a wooden voice.

The time it took him to reply, and the unnatural tone of his voice did not go unnoticed, but what Kachem made of it Dorn could not tell.

189

"Hollie's not answering her phone," the Major said.

Dorn stared back, unmoved.

"I guess she's on the job, which can't be said about you." Kachem's voice was sober, biting.

Dorn breathed in with relief. It was the Kachem he knew. The man could not let a moment slip by without making innuendos, scalding, always in search of a rat, ready to flush one out—

Dorn froze. Suddenly he was stricken with an idea. He may have found just the right conclusion to Maj. Kachem's woes.

"What have you been doing?" the visitor pressed.

"I'm closing in," Dorn replied with a sudden spark in his eyes.

"The mole? You know who!" Kachem's voice was entirely sober now, filled with as much surprise as with hope.

"I have a pretty good idea," Dorn said.

"Tell me!"

He was not ready. He needed time to grow the thought which had only just set seed.

"I need time," he said.

Kachem snarled at the suggestion, but understood the need to fine-tune an operation.

"We should work together—"

"No!— I mean, I need time to set it up. The locals can spoil it—."

"Ha! You needn't worry about it anymore!" Kachem exclaimed with cockiness.

"We don't want the locals botching the operation. We want the courier to leave this place alive, don't we?"

"As I said — they won't dare interfere anymore."

Dorn wanted to part with the man, but felt it was important to play to Kachem's vanity.

"How's that?" he asked absentmindedly.

"They received a reminder of who gives orders in this Godforsaken place! We train their military officers, we supply their weaponry, intelligence, and fund their elections. We are de facto in charge."

"Nothing to be proud of—" Dorn started and bit his tongue.

"Huh?"

He felt Kachem's piercing eyes prick his skin. The sensation roused him, reminded to stay on guard.

"Our disciples give us little reason to be proud," he corrected.

Kachem's gaze hung on Dorn's face for an uncomfortably long time.

"Yes," the Major said at last. "Killing of the brother was inexcusable. They're brutes who lack finesse that is required to spar with the Company. We've allowed them to become confident in the might that protects them. They operate on the level of a small-town bully. They don't understand that in this day and age no power, however big, can underestimate the hearts and minds of the people it wants to liberate. The Company, for all its vile teaching, has an enormous following in this part of the world. To kill their own, and in the way it was conducted, could set us back years. Worse — it could rekindle the following the Company has not enjoyed since the killing of the Archbishop. Which is why we must act quickly. The sooner we complete the mission, the sooner we'll bring down the Company. And the best is it'll collapse on its own, without us taking the heat for it."

"We must act quickly," Dorn agreed. In his mind he added, 'I must act quickly.'

"What you have going?"

"I have a plan—"

"You said it, already, Dorn! I want results!"

"As you said — we must act with finesse. Keep the locals off my back, and you'll have the mission completed by tonight—"

39. Doubts

Dorn breathed in with relief. Having Kachem off his back even for several hours could mean the difference between life and death. He did not waste the time so providentially afforded him. Picking the lock was a simple matter, but doing it without raising the attention of the inhabitant was something else. To create a level of surprise he dialed a number for the reception. He began to work on the lock the moment the call was transferred and he heard the telephone ring inside. The diversion worked. The lock gave in, and he entered the room in time to catch the woman unawares.

"Don't do it, Hollie!" he warned.

She was standing over the bedside table, her back turned to the entrance door, her eyes on the ringing telephone, one hand inside a purse. The fact she did not react more quickly was the result of hearing the sound of the familiar voice, a voice, which should not be heard from again.

It was all Dorn required. He approached in three leaps, his hand grasping the hand in the purse. He drew out a small pistol.

The woman did not resist. Her body wilted like a chipmunk caught under a hat. She was caught by a surprise too great to react, or to speak. What could she say, anyway? What explanation could she offer? Here stood a man whom she had slated to disappear at a remote internment camp in the mountains.

Dorn was as surprised by the development as the woman. He did not expect to find her this easily. Hope? Yes, he hoped, and hope propelled his actions, but to see her again, when he expected her to disappear far and away, was indeed a grand surprise. Now that she was within his arm's reach, under his command, he did not know how to proceed. He was at a loss. His body firmly pressed against the woman, pinning her to the wall, his mind racing, he breathed into her ear. What should he do? He could not bring himself to coerce her. He doubted she would ever give in, anyway. She was a professional in a line of work, which prepared for all extreme eventualities. Of one thing he was certain, though. Whatever had to happen, could not be done under the nose of the sneaky Maj. Kachem.

He loosened his grip.

"We're going!" he said.

Overwhelmed by the sudden change in her situation the woman did not react. A firm nudge prompted her to move. She walked on stiff legs, the barrel of the pistol pressed to her kidney, directing her toward the door. Passing the minuscule dresser in the narrow hallway, Dorn picked up a wide woolen shawl the woman had purchased from a street vendor. He hung it over his arm to conceal the pistol, and opened the door.

Not wanting to run into Kachem, Dorn descended to the ground level, and directed the woman toward the restaurant. Early diners occupied the best tables, lazily watching the plaza where street musicians were readying for the evening's entertainment. Dorn led the woman between tables. She reacted to his silent prompts with resignation. A single row of tables separated them from the exit onto the plaza, when Dorn froze at the sound of the one person whose voice he did not want to hear.

"You two look like you're onto something!"

Maj. Kachem rose up from the wicker chair he freshly occupied, as evidenced by an as yet untouched glass of alcohol in his hand.

Dorn's mind worked frantically. He felt the woman stiffen. He pressed the barrel into her kidney.

"I think you ought to tell me what you're up to," Kachem said unconvincingly, his will battling between the temptation of the drink, and the desire for a successful completion of the mission.

"Order a bottle of whatever you're having, and we'll join you… soon," Dorn said in a voice which suggested a reward.

"You'll bring the mole?"

"On a silver platter."

The woman glanced at her captor. Her eyes were puzzled, but sparkled, which told Dorn she had at last returned to her senses. Not wanting to lose the benefit of the upper hand he nudged her, and led her away without turning back. They hurried away, leaving the baffled officer no time to react. They crossed the plaza, and turned sharply behind the cathedral, where Dorn hailed a taxi.

He was just as surprised as the woman when he gave the driver the direction. What did he hope to achieve by returning to the volcano? Chances were the courier met the fate bestowed upon Brother Anselm, despite Kachem's assurances, Chief del Toro's words still ringing in his head. Indeed, Maj. Kachem was fooling himself thinking he won over the local overlords' desire to destroy the Company in the way practiced by all brutal regimes of the region. However big was the might that bankrolled and militarily supported the Junta, its influence was limited, for the puppet regimes quickly learned of the power they wielded over their strongest ally. Surrounded by states turning decidedly hostile toward the Superpower, they remained the bases from which their benefactor operated in the region. In effect, they commanded the rules of cooperation, however seldom enforced. Indeed, nothing could stop the Junta from rounding and assassinating every member of the Company, if it should wish so. Universally condemned around the world for the way they treated own citizens, they were no longer bound by rules of engagement with the international community. Secure in the conviction of unconditional support from their ally they conducted their domestic policy as seen fit. Dorn understood it, and expected the worst. The only thing left for him was to confront the woman in the most dramatic way he could think of. The house on the slopes of the volcano was where he last saw the courier alive. It would be the last place the woman herself would see.

The woman's persistent silence suggested she knew what fate awaited her. Dorn felt her anxiety rise with every curve of the steep road that brought them closer to the inevitable conclusion. Her breath became shallow, her fingers intertwined on her thighs, creating nervous and uncontrollable figures. He found satisfaction in her suffering. It eased his desire to deliver immediate punishment. He was not proud of the emotion, but made no effort to suppress it. He did not want to.

Dorn's emotions reached their peak when he pushed the woman ahead of him, down the familiar path, which originated on the side of the road, and descended to the green oasis.

"Have you any idea what you're getting yourself into?" the woman spoke for the first time when they reached the first fork in the path. Her voice was laced with remorse.

"It did not have to come to this," he said icily.

It did not! he reiterated in his mind. Brother Anselm and the courier did not have to die. It was perverse and unnecessary cruelty.

She turned around to face him. Her eyes glistened.

It enraged him. He nudged her with the barrel, forced to continue on.

"Too late for remorse. Yours and mine!"

He said it in as cruel a voice as he could muster. He did not want to admit to himself how these eyes affected him. These were the eyes he saw the night of drinking, dancing, and telling stories. A careless night when something happened, when his heart was moved. It was the night when they were no longer two officers on a clandestine mission. They were a man and a woman, close together, bound by the most wonderful of human emotions. He did not dare name it now. It would not do. What had to be done had to be done. Yet, he could not help the pins in his heart. These eyes looked directly into his heart. They reminded him of the attractive human being, of the closeness they enjoyed for a brief moment in time, of the gentle and compassionate woman underneath the skin of a demon. But these eyes reminded him of something else. The night Brother Anselm was killed she arrived to meet Dorn and Kachem, and her eyes glistened as they did just now. Was it remorse for having caused the cruel and painful death? Perhaps it was a sign she was not as devoid of human emotions as was expected of someone of her profession? Perhaps her frequent contact, through assignments, with the Company and other sympathetic Orders involved in the same struggle had affected her, as it often happens to one who is exposed to the ways of a morally superior opponent. Did Capt. Weader see the light? Was a seed planted in her mind and heart? Could he converted her?

Dorn was dumbstruck by the thought. It started to burrow through his mind. What would Brother Anselm do? he asked himself. And the answer was clear, the only answer that came to mind. Was it not his duty, as a member of the Order famous for its missionary work, to facilitate the conversion?

Dorn looked at the figure of the woman who proceeded him, with different eyes. She walked tall, proud, ready to face the only just outcome of her actions. Here was an officer of the gravest enemy the Company ever faced, and Dorn was having doubts about the necessary response. What did he want? What were his plans? He had questions, but no answers.

Circumstances provided the answers for him.

They crossed the clearing, undisturbed, and followed the green pasture toward the buildings. From a distance they could see the stables and the house, and soon they could make out some figures between the buildings. Dorn recognized the guards who watched him in the stables. Their backs turned to the newcomers, they were engaged in an animated discussion. As Dorn neared he realized the guards were not talking to each other, but to someone else, who until now remained invisible, hidden behind the open gate of the stables.

"Perhaps her telephone is switched off?" said one of the guards in his guttural Spanish.

"Or she has fallen into the hands of this beast" added the second. "No woman can endure the kind of torture the old Brother did. She will talk—"

"She will," seconded the first man. "Which is why you must leave immediately."

The man they were addressing stepped forward from behind the gate, and placed his hands on both men's shoulders. He said something quietly and reassuringly to the guards but Dorn could not understand the words. He was shocked by the identity of the man he did not expect to see alive.

40. Verification

A rustle behind their backs roused the guards. They reacted swiftly, their automatics aimed at Dorn.

"No! Pedro y Pablo!" the elderly man cried with authority capable of stopping bullets.

The guards wavered. They kept aim, their faces expressing hatred but, perhaps because of the woman who proceeded Dorn and was in the line of fire, or perhaps out of obedience, which was stronger than dogged human emotions, they did not fire.

Having surmised the guards were in control of their emotions Dorn stepped forward. In passing the woman their eyes locked for a brief moment. Something peculiar flickered in Hollie Weader's the deep blue gaze. He detected no concern for her fate. Her tenacity impressed him. What gave her the confidence? Was it arrogance? He detected none. What he saw in those beautiful eyes was peaceful self-confidence. Where it came from he could not fathom, but he knew it would not last, for he was ready to expose her.

Dorn reached underneath his shirt and yanked angrily. He extracted a silver chain, and threw it to the elderly man who caught it with unexpected agility.

"Verify my identity!" Dorn nodded to the chain, at the end of which hung a silver cross.

He gazed back at the woman and was satisfied at her reaction. Capt. Weader's face turned as pale as the silver the cross was made of.

If the elderly man was surprised he did not show it. He glanced into Dorn's eyes, then into the woman's. He reached into his breast pocket and drew out a pair of slim reading glasses. The crease between his eyebrows deepened as he studied the encrusted cross with utmost concentration.

Dorn could not help but express his satisfaction out loud.

"It's authentic, unlike whatever this— impostor used to gain your confidence, Father."

Dorn triumphed. He knew his bona fide was irreproachable. He wore it everyday of his life since presented with it by Brother Anselm. His mind ventured back to the day it happened...

"With this cross you officially join the community of the Invisible Company," Brother Anselm said. "It is as unique as you are. It identifies you as one of us. It opens doors to any facility owned or operated by the Company."

"What prevents someone from copying it?" Dorn asked with naivety of his young age.

Brother Anselm turned the cross over.

"In the event that you should lose it, or it is taken from you by force, it contains a key unique to you."

"Where?" Dorn did not see.

"You're looking at it."

He could not see any distinctive marks.

"This— floral design?"

"It isn't merely a design. It is a cryptograph, which unlocks your personal file in the Company's main vault computer. It allows us to identify the bearer in case of doubt."

"Can I read it?"

"In time you will learn to read the cryptograph. It may become a matter of life and death."

"What is it?"

Brother Anselm smiled.

"It is our closest-guarded secret. This is how we communicate."

"But can't it be decrypted?"

"It is one of but a handful of unbroken codes in existence. It came to our possession centuries ago, and has survived the test of time."

"And no one knows about it?"

"Oh, it is quite well known, even famous. It is, arguably, the most famous code of all."

"How can this be?"

"People have studied it for centuries, countless cryptologists tried to break it, and all have failed."

"Do you mean to say that it is available for others to study?"

"Naturally. It is a manuscript, a work of an artist. It belongs in the cultural domain for all humanity to enjoy."

"Forgive me, Brother Anselm, but you are talking in riddles. How can it be known and famous, and remain a closest-guarded secret, simultaneously?"

"The secret is the key to unlock the code, and the Company possesses the key, without which it remains but a beautiful, if mysterious work of art."

"How can you be certain the code has never been broken?"

"Our Fathers created a close derivative of the code contained in the manuscript. For a long time locked up in the vaults of an Italian monastery, the original was sold in the early 20th century to a rare book dealer. Since then countless minds have tried to crack it, and our Fathers have kept close eyes on the attempts. By releasing the manuscript to the world our Fathers made a brilliant move. Open competitions, a very public race to break the code, are the best guarantors that success will become widely known."

"Has it not happened?"

"You and thousands of our members would not be wearing it on your necks if it had."

Dorn looked closer at the encrusted cross, its intricate design becoming blurry, causing his eyes to strain.

"You say that I will learn to decrypt the code?"

"You must learn it. Your survival depends upon it."

"But it means that so can our enemies."

"Not without access to the original document, which is now, and shall forever remain in the vaults of the Company. You see, each cross contains a tiny fragment of the original manuscript. Those of our members whose task requires them to wear the cross, are given access to the source document. They study it, they commit it to memory. When the time comes to verify the authenticity of another Brother's cross they must evoke the document from memory. They find the fragment, a piece of the puzzle, and place it precisely within the document, all within their mind."

Now, years later, Dorn smiled. It was a simple, yet ingenious device. He used it to confirm the identity of members of the Company, as others used it to verify his. It required concentration, mental discipline every Brother and Father acquired in the course of his training. It was the sort of concentration the silver-haired courier mustered right now.

Evidently the verification process went in Dorn's favor as the courier extended his arms and the two men embraced.

Dorn could not help but turn around to show the woman his triumphant face. What he saw on hers was not what he expected. From the deep blue eyes poured heavy silver tears.

41. Agents of Change

The two guards watched in stupefaction as the man they would have killed was received with fraternal embrace. They were not privy to the secrets of the Brothers and Fathers whom they served, though served them they did with all their hearts. Grudgingly, mindful of the humiliating defeat suffered earlier in the day from the unarmed man, they accepted now the decision of the Father whose safety they were responsible for. Though earlier deemed the enemy, by some mysterious force the newcomer was welcomed into the inner circle, he became one of them. They lowered their weapons, but their faces remained sharp, their eyes vigilant.

"Why don't we talk in private?" Dorn turned to the courier, his eyes motioning the guards. "I'd rather they did not know too much about me," he added confidentially.

The stately Father lead him several steps away, into the last remaining rays of the low, setting sun. They faced each other.

"This woman is a spy," Dorn said without much ado. "She is impersonating one of our captured agents."

The elderly man seemed to grow slowly as his back straightened.

"I see," he said, his face expressionless. He turned to the woman and waived her in with an inviting gesture.

"Repeat what you just told me," he said to Dorn, when the woman approached.

Dorn hesitated. Something was not right. The courier did not appear surprised by his disclosure. Not a muscle twitched on his creased face. Not one eyelid blinked. And the woman? She carried herself proudly. Her eyes, while glistening with tears, were smiling. She looked into the face of the old man with daughterly trust. Then into Dorn's, with placid amusement. Change in her countenance was the most astounding. It confused Dorn. Then it terrified him. Did he make a mistake? Was it possible the courier was not the courier at all?

Slowly, Dorn retreated one step. Then another. And another. All along his eyes darted between the elder and the woman.

"Relax!" the gentle voice caught him the moment his right hand reached into the small of his back where the small pistol lay behind his belt. "I am Father Giordano, the courier you are looking for." He extended his arm and the woman approached. He slipped his arm underneath hers, and said, "I don't believe you were *properly* introduced. Please meet Capt. Hollie Weader, the notorious mole-buster, and a valuable member of the Invisible Company."

Dorn was stunned.

"No!" he cried.

His eyes darted between the two. Their embrace was natural and trusting as only long friendship could evoke. When could such long friendship have been built? Dorn wondered in horror.

He retreated yet another step, and cried, "No! It cannot be! She is lying! She is an impostor!" And so are you, he wanted to add.

The man shook his head, his hypnotically pacifying eyes set on Dorn's.

"Hollie's identity is beyond doubt. I've known her since she was born."

Dorn shivered suddenly as the woman reached underneath her blouse, and extracted a silver chain. She pulled the chain over her head, and tossed it to Dorn.

Dorn caught it midair. The chain was similar to his, and adorned with a familiar silver cross. He glanced at it but could not muster the concentration required to study the ingrained code.

"Take your time," the old man said gently.

It took several attempts, his eyes unable to focus, constantly wanting to shoot back to the pair.

At last, his face pale, Dorn said, "But this is not the cross —" he paused.

"Of course not," the woman said. This is not the fake which Kachem equipped both of us with, and which would not have allowed a pass to sacristy, let alone entry to the inner circle of the courier."

True enough, in his hands was the authentic cross, with the authentic piece of the puzzle that was the code. It was not the cross he and the woman were given as part of their false identity. He carried his fake in his pocket, never intending to use it, convinced that the same would expose the woman when she attempted to pass on for an envoy of the Company. He was surprised she was able to gain the confidence of the local network with what should have led to her immediate exposure. Not only did she penetrate the extraordinary security measures undertaken by the network, but managed to fool the emissary of the Company's high command. The only explanation to the unbelievable scenario he could think of was the impossible: the unbreakable, the source code, which served as the Company's cryptograph, its closest-guarded possession, had been compromised. It was the only explanation behind the authentic cross she presented him with. Its porous surface burned his hand.

"How— How is this possible?" he uttered.

"Come," the elderly extended his free arm. "Let us go inside. You are owed an explanation.

The house, though small, was spacious chiefly due to sparse furnishings. Kept in an immaculate condition by members of the Invisible Company, its official cover was that of a small farm house belonging to a Mercado vendor who sold his crop in the city. In reality the crop, from chickens and ducks, to field greens, was grown and harvested by young men and women to provide for the members of the Company who traveled the country incognito. Two of such young people were in the house, preparing the evening meal.

Seated around a long and simple wooden dining table, still dazed by the change about, Dorn was reintroduced to the woman whom he knew under a different name.

"My true name is Elizabeth Evelyn," she said as soon as they settled down. "My parents were physicians with Doctors without Borders, they volunteered to treat the victims of war ravaged regions, the landless *campesinos*, the orphaned, the widowed—"

Her voice broke with emotion, and the courier took over. He spoke in a low voice, his hand on the woman's, comforting, adding courage.

"Lizzie's parents perished in a death squad raid. The entire field hospital was burned, along with all the sick and wounded. Someone hid the little girl, and she watched the horror from a hole in the ground, literally, for it was an improvised refrigerator filled with dry ice and medicines. She was found none too late by our supply team, on the verge of hypercapnia, caused by prolonged exposure to dry ice."

"Has… no one else survived?" Dorn asked with a lump in his throat, the account closely resembling that of his own transformational experience.

"The death squads operate on the principle to leave no witnesses. No one survived, save for the terrified little girl."

Dorn looked at the woman, sorrow in his eyes.

"We—" he started. "We've a lot in common." In short broken sentences he told his story.

"A civil war brought the both of you to join the force for change," the courier concluded.

Overwhelmed, Dorn watched the man and the woman for some time, speechless.

Then he said in a low, sorrowful voice, "Ours are only two of countless lives affected by the evil of the few who unleash misery on entire populations. The two of us joined the Invisible Company to bring about change, but what have we achieved? Look around, Father Giordano. The country is at a brink of yet another civil war. Is change attainable at all?"

"Both of you worked relentlessly to bring about change. You and thousands of our professed, as well as lay brother and sisters. You are making a difference."

"We were not able to stop the spread of evil. Another brutal war may break out any day—"

"You are making a difference! You are the difference! You are agents of change. Your work reaches directly into the hearts of all who are affected by violence and oppression."

"It's hard to see the effect of our work with violence breaking out all around—"

"You mustn't lose faith!"

"Faith? It isn't my faith I worry about, for I have chosen a path from which I shall not stray. I worry about those who placed their faith in us, only to see us powerless to effect change—"

"Violence may appear to be winning by its shear, brutal nature, which affects everyone. What you do is chip away its effects by reaching into the hearts of the affected, one by one. It is a long process, which cannot happen overnight, as opposed to wars which erupt quickly. But change is coming.

We are now working on all levels of the social and political ladder. Our agents are present in the corridors of power, advising those who are in the position to wage, or stop wars. Too, we are among the grassroots, in base communities, in the smallest of villages, where we teach love and practical skills. The latter empower the poorest of the poor to find jobs. Examples abound. We give people hope, we show them a better world is possible—"

"It only angers the high and mighty who take it out on the meager!"

"There are two kinds of people who vie for positions of power. There are the sociopaths who are fueled by the misery they cause to others. And then there are the basic careerists. We cannot help the former; the only solution is to remove them from society. But the latter, and these are the majority, we can help to see the way. Rise on the social ladder doesn't have to be achieved on the backs of the poor. Our agents are in the offices of policymakers, from advising residents to taking on cabinet positions, as many did across the world. Change is not only coming, it is already here and it is making headways. Look at the neighboring countries, look at the other, further south, who adopted social policies unthinkable in this region previously dominated by fascist dictators. We are making a difference, Kamil. We are."

They sat quietly for a time, their spirits lifted by the impassioned speech, and the smells coming from the kitchen where the two guards women were busy preparing a meal for the courier and his guests.

"I am so very sorry about the— the dreadful mistake," the woman opened.

Dorn played down the misunderstanding and its effects.

"Oh, it's nothing. I'm used to being roughed up." He shifted uncomfortably in his seat, and added, "I must confess something, too. I was convinced you were responsible for Brother Anselm's capture, his death—"

"Ah! It's so dreadful what happened!" the woman covered her eyes with the palm of her hand.

207

"How did it happen?" Dorn wondered out loud.

"The Opus Dei intercepted a coded message sent from the Building—" the courier replied.

"It was I—" he said in a broken voice.

"You couldn't've prevented it. They were onto Brother Anselm for decades. He was marked since that night in 1989, when he survived, while his friends were assassinated."

"I would gladly give my life to save his!"

"You mustn't think this way, Kamil. If we all did it for our brothers and sisters, then who would be left to do our work? You must go on."

Now that he started he could not stop, and words poured out of him. He spoke of his doubts, his fears, and his hopes.

"I thought I was marked," Dorn went on. "I was convinced Kachem chose me for this mission only to expose me. That night when he arrived here in town I thought I was finished—"

"But I thought the same!" the woman cried. "For some time now I was convinced you— they were onto me. And this operation especially. Your camaraderie with the man who caught Karin Platt—"

"Brother Anselm."

She nodded.

"I recognized him at the airport right away. It was the man whose sketch I saw and committed to memory. Then I saw you fraternizing on the plane, and again in the city. I thought it was a ruse, and he a plant sent to break my cover. How could I have guessed that he and you—? I panicked. I lost my head. I thought it safest to play along as though I noticed nothing. But you— You and he just kept on crossing my path. Last time in the cathedral."

"Did you—? Was it you—?" His voice broke.

"No, of course not! I did not know he really was one of us until it was too late. When Kachem called me that night of the murder, I thought you were the one who sold him out to those butchers. I wanted to— I wanted to do you harm."

Dorn dug into her eyes. They were glistening but somber, not garnished with remorse. He did not expect to find it. He felt the same way about her. He wished the same to the one he suspected of exposing Brother Anselm to the monsters who killed him. He would have delivered his own justice to the one who caused his friend's death. Perhaps he still may.

Dorn told them who killed Brother Anselm. He told them about the massacre in the Sierra Madres.

"I will not rest until Chief del Toro pays for his crimes. However long it takes. Whatever it takes. I will find him."

The woman and the courier exchanged glances.

"You mustn't, Kamil," the courier said quietly. "The guilty build their own destiny. No bad deed goes unpunished, but it is not for us to deliver punishment."

'Tis the difference between you and me, Father, Dorn thought. 'Tis why you took the final vows and became a professed Father, while I chose the path which promised temporal punishment.

He said nothing. No words could describe the thousand images that shot through his head, and which concentrated into one word. Murder. He could murder, right now, right here. He could kill the man who was responsible for the death of Brother Anselm. He could murder him in a thousand ways, delivering elaborate pain, prolonging the suffering of the one who deserved to suffer the same pain he caused to his countless victims.

"The loss of Brother Anselm is immeasurable," the courier broke Dorn's silent reverie. "We must not forget he laid down his life for a better world. He wasn't alone. Many of our brothers and sisters died for change, many will give their lives still, and each sacrifice will become a new drop in a sea of hope for the countless who suffer. Let us pray for the light that guided the three of us to a safe reunion. Let us give thanks for sparing the lives of the two of you." His eyes dived deep into the eyes of his companions. "You must go on, come what may. You and others like you are the only hope for too many."

He prayed, his arms across the table, his hands on the hands of the young man and woman who were the hopes of many. He prayed for the lives of those who laid their lives, and those who continued to risk theirs. He finished with words, which made Dorn freeze, "And let us pray for the one who is in grave danger as we speak. Let us pray that he does not meet the fate bestowed on Brother Anselm."

Father Giordano sensed sudden change in Dorn. He turned to his young companion.

"Kamil?"

"Of whom are you speaking, Father?" Dorn asked.

"Why, I am speaking of the mole your Maj. Kachem hunts. The one who picked up the item from Karin Platt. He is, doubtless, lonely, scared, lost among the enemy— Brother Anselm dispatched a coded message after Karin Platt's capture. He let us know of the death of an old Brother who was a go-between, who delivered to us documents procured by Platt. He received them from a deep cover agent, who worked at the military headquarters—"

"And who goes by the codename Ichneumon," Dorn broke in.

They looked at him, puzzled.

"I am Ichneumon. I am the deep cover agent you speak of."

Capt. Hollie Weader, aka Elizabeth Evelyn, sprung to her feet.

"You!?"

She observed him wide-eyed.

Dorn reached into his trousers' pocket, and presented them with a small object he held between his thumb and index finger.

42. Thirst for Blood

The excitement subsided eventually. Sober thoughts returned.

"I hope it was worth the loss of our two brothers, and Karin Platt," Dorn thought out loud while weighing the digital drive in his hand.

Father Giordano understood.

"You are owed yet another explanation," he said. He nodded to the small device in Dorn's hand and continued, "This should never have occurred, but we live in a world where not even diplomatic immunity is observed. The digital drive was stolen from a diplomatic pouch belonging to our courier while he was en route from Rome to our Provincials. A mistake was made — the drive was not properly encrypted, and is vulnerable. It contains enough material to reconstruct our code. Was retrieving it worth the sacrifice? Should our enemies have succeeded in breaking the code they would have had open access to our servers. In essence — they would've been able to wreak immeasurable damage

211

on the scale similar to cyber attacks conducted by the nation states."

"What about the fake digital drive? The Trojan Horse Capt. Weader— Elizabeth brought from the Building?"

The courier waved his hand dismissively.

"Child's play. It would have worked only if they had broken the original code."

"Have they not?"

"The trouble is we cannot tell. There are unaccounted-for hours, and we cannot rule out that the code was copied, and their cryptologists are working on decryption as we speak, however—"

"What does it mean, then?" the woman cut him off, anxiously.

"What I was trying to say, is that our own estimates suggest it would take years to break the code based on the material available on the drive, which would give us time to issue new codes. The truth, however, is that we cannot rule out the possibility that at some point more samples were appropriated, and the code contained on the digital drive was... a sort of a missing link necessary to reconstruct the whole."

"It served us so well, for so long," Dorn said after due silence.

The courier nodded.

"Centuries in its original form, and another century in its derivative. It outlived any expectations, but we mustn't fret over it. Sooner or later all codes succumb to decryption. We should rejoice that our enemy made a mistake. Their brute attack warned us. It could have been much worse had they acted with finesse that was practiced in the old days of espionage. We would not have known and carried on as if nothing happened."

"What will happen when nothing happens?" Dorn asked.

This time the courier seemed caught off-guard.

"I mean to Hollie— Elizabeth—"

"Let's stick to Hollie for now," the woman suggested with a gentle smile. "I'd hate it if my name slipped out in front of Kachem."

Dorn smiled.

"I meant what will happen, now that Hollie is expected to deliver the fake drive to the courier, to you, Father Giordano?"

The courier thought about it before replying.

"We shall have to come up with something in order to reasonably satisfy Maj. Kachem as to Hollie's successful completion of her mission. Meanwhile there is a more pressing issue. This Maj. Kachem wants the mole who extracted the drive from the Building."

"And he will not rest until he gets him! Whatever we may think of his brute tactic, one thing remains undeniable — Kachem usually gets what he wants." The woman's eyes landed on Dorn's.

"It is true," Dorn said. "Kachem must be satisfied here and now."

They each fell silent for a time, each pondering the question of how to satisfy Maj. Kachem's hunger for blood.

"I admit, I am at a loss," Dorn said at last. He finished with a bashful look in his eyes, "I rather thought I would find a way to convince Kachem you were the mole."

The woman returned the look.

"I thought something to that effect about you."

"Perhaps, then," said Father Giordano," Brother Anselm could make another, this time a post-mortem sacrifice?"

They looked at him, puzzled.

"Brother Anselm was Karin Platt's recruiter," continued the courier. "His whereabouts can be traced to the night Karin stole the drive. His death at the hands of the brutal Chief del Toro may give us the opportunity to create rift between the Superpower and the local Junta. We may plant a suggestion whereby the original drive was appropriated by the torturers—"

"No!" Dorn shook his head. "It's a good idea but it won't fly. Something would always haunt Kachem — Brother Anselm could not have accessed the Building to extract the drive, which means that there still exists a mole on the inside. Besides, Kachem is already sniffing around me. I can feel it. He suspects me of killing Fink, does he not?"

The woman blushed.

"What happened to this man Fink was regrettable, but unavoidable," the courier said. "Pedro and Pablo accompanied Hollie as her backup. Remember we thought Fink was going to expose Hollie as the mole. Fink was a snitch. Worse — he was a mercenary during the civil war, a paid killer who served with death squads. He had it coming one way or another, if not in this than in afterlife. He had a pistol that night. He was ready to use it. Pedro acted quickly. It is no use to belabor it now. What's done is done. Let us move on."

Three sets of eyes gazed from face to face. No words were exchanged for a time.

"We can transfer you to one of our missions where Maj. Kachem's vindictive sword does not reach," the courier suggested at last.

"No!" Dorn objected vehemently. "I can do so much more in my position."

"You can achieve nothing if you become exposed. On the other hand you can continue to work for the cause in any of our base communities, using an assumed identity."

"I can do the same in the Building, even if I can convert one more soul, that's one more on our side—"

"Kamil—" the courier tried.

"It would mean a terrible a setback, if the Company sent me away. Replacing an agent in my position would take years. I'm not a quitter who abandons his brothers at first sign of trouble."

"You're not a quitter, but you are too valuable to lose," the woman said gently.

"Your dedication is admirable, Kamil, but it must go hand in hand with practical application. Returning to the Building may cost you more than Maj. Kachem's suspicious glances. It may not end with superficial bruises, either—" Father Giordano pointed to the scabs on Dorn's arms and face.

Dorn was dumbstruck.

"Bruises!" he cried.

He touched the scars on his face, blood rushing to his head. His eyes glistened with a peculiar mixture of hope and vindictive satisfaction.

"Of course! Why haven't I thought about it sooner?"

They looked at him, not understanding. Their friend appeared mad.

"You do not need to give yourself up for torture to prove you are worthy!" the woman said in a broken voice.

Dorn set his hand on hers. His eyes sent bright sparks of enthusiasm.

"I was struck with a solution. I think we might be able to satisfy Maj. Kachem's thirst for blood."

A plan emerged in his mind. He explained.

43. Prepping the Scene

"What if Kachem doesn't fall for it?" Elizabeth Evelyn, aka Capt. Hollie Weader asked for the nth time.

They were sitting on a park bench on Plaza Catedral, diagonally from the restaurant where Maj. Kachem shared a table with an elderly gentleman. The two men were chatting, laughing, raising glasses to each other. A bottle on the table was nearly half drank, and Dorn assessed the officer was sufficiently intoxicated, but not too drunk to carry on with the plan devised for his benefit.

The woman had her doubts still. After several minutes of rehashing the risky plan she expressed her concerns about the ad hoc way in which the plan was devised. Being an intelligence officer she was used to meticulous planning, where room for chance did not exist, yet chance was what Dorn was counting on the most.

"If I read him correctly, and I believe I know Maj. Kachem enough to allow for such a conclusion, I think he will fall for it," Dorn replied as assuredly as he could. "His pent up agitation and hunger for the mole is such that Kachem will not be able to contain the shock of the moment. Thus, what remains for us, is to stage a convincing enough play."

"Precisely!" She caught on to the thought, her doubts not giving way easily. "There's enough here to make you wonder if we can pull it off, from your psychological evaluation of the target, to our ability to time it as precisely as your plan requires."

"The plan is underway already," Dorn replied irritably, but checked himself. He understood the woman's hesitation. It was not so much doubt, as it was her own pent up tension that made her insist that he repeat over and over every detail of the plan, and look for the slightest weak points. "If you worked with Kachem as closely as I, you'd understand him better. I saw it in his eyes. I heard it in his voice. I know what drives him. It allows me to predict his most likely reaction when presented with a set of events—"

"But so many variables that can go wrong!"

"Most of them won't matter, not when the eyes see what the heart desires."

Dorn checked his wristwatch. At the same time his mobile phone vibrated in his pocket. He answered it and listened with concentration. He ended the connection and turned to the woman.

"Pablo and Pedro are ready."

She clenched her jaws before replying.

"This is it, then."

Her eyes glided toward the restaurant and the small table where Maj. Kachem was passing the time awaiting promised resolution.

"I so hope to God he is ready, too," she added with a deep sigh.

"Relax. Give Father Giordano some credit. He's doing a great job. Look!"

217

She gazed to the restaurant table again. She saw Maj. Kachem and the elderly click their glasses, and down the contents in one swig.

"You and I, we're lay people, but Father Giordano— I do not envy him. How can he reconcile what we've planned, with his religious beliefs?"

"You and I share those beliefs, too, and while neither of us likes what must be done, I think we both agree that in a hopeless case such as this the punishment must fit the crime."

She looked into his eyes. He found in them no contradiction.

"Father Giordano mustn't know what really transpired," she said quietly.

"He won't if all goes according to the plan."

They looked again to the small table and the two men who occupied it. They had observed them for close to an hour now. One of the men was dressed in a large cowboy hat, a colorful shirt with imprints of galloping horses, a glistening belt buckle and imitation snake skin boots. He was a spitting image of a farmer spending an evening on the town, drinking, chatting, listening to street music. His behavior betrayed a jovial man, who appeared to know everyone, bowing and chatting up passersby, and singing under his breath to the tunes played by the guitar player who took up a position in front of the restaurant. At first occupying a single table, he soon drew the attention of Maj. Kachem and, little by little, imposed himself on the lone Gringo. Kachem felt neither the need nor did he object to the company of the colorful man. He did not mind raising a glass to help pass the time, and as the timepiece on the nearby city hall clicked minutes so did the shot glasses. With every rising of the wrist Kachem's eyes lost their inextricable sharpness, his facial features smoothed, and his voice timbre lost the urgency that was his trait.

The alcohol reinforced with a mild relaxant slipped into the glass at a moment of inattention, its effect strengthened by climate shock, did what Father Giordano was waiting for. He gave a silent signal to his two companions whose anticipation was stretched to the limits.

"Kachem is ready," Dorn said upon noticing the prearranged signal.

44. Diversion

"I can't remember the last time I was this nervous before an operation," Hollie confessed.

Her short statement told more about the woman than Dorn could have hoped to learn in the course of the longest interrogation. It cut through the air as a whip, dismissing any lingering notions of the ruthless and heartless beast he had associated her with only hours earlier, and exposed a vulnerable woman who was not devoid of basic human emotions. An image of a monstrous enemy was replaced with that of a compassionate friend whose paths in life ran parallel to Dorn's. Seeing her lower lip tremble he realized he ought to do something to offer reassurance.

Dorn knew how crucial were the minutes that preceded an operation, when every detail put an enormous weight on the anxious mind. He placed his hand on hers and said in order to keep her mind occupied in those last minutes before the plan commenced, "Tell me something about yourself."

A spark in her eyes said she appreciated the effort.

"What you mean? Like for a yearbook?"

"Something personal. Anything."

"Why not?" she said, her eyes on an unspecified point in the crown of the laurel tree that formed an umbrella over their heads. "It wasn't really the death of my parents that made me join the Invisible Company. Sure, I grieved, but remember I was only a child. Life went on. I was no different from my girlfriends, I wanted to have fun. The substitute family was good to me, they loved me, and soon they became my parents. I grew up as most kids do. I went to high school, then college. Then I met him— I was nineteen. He was twenty five. I suppose a psychologist would make the case that I needed someone closer than my adopted family, which would explain why we married within months of meeting. The truth, though, was that I loved him, and he loved me. Then, not long after the wedding, he was sent to a warzone—"

"A soldier?"

"A photojournalist. After years of doing menial jobs for a local community paper he was suddenly offered a major gig for a big national. We talked about it. I had my college exams coming, and we decided he could go away for a few months, while I finished school. He never came back."

"I'm sorry."

She did not acknowledge the words of sympathy, aware she might break down if she did. She continued without looking at her companion, "The Fathers offered counseling. They were good at it. They helped me get back on my feet and finish the degree. And later I did not need much convincing to join the Invisible Company in order to help end wars."

Dorn could imagine how the young woman's mind worked at the time, her situation paralleling his. Both were struck by the horror of war, and at this impressionable and tender age when one does not need a great deal of convincing that a change is attainable, a must. He could still hear Brother Anselm's words reverberate in his ears, "Join us and help implode the beast from within."

The woman confirmed his thoughts.

"They said the best, the bloodless way, to change the way of the evil, was to join its ranks, to convert every soldier, one at a time. They said such an approach not only eliminates a set of hands that hold a gun, but when combined with active missionary work and education it gains another soul to our cause. I helped recruit men and women to our side, the side of change, just as the Fathers predicted, one soldier at a time."

"But you've become a notorious legend. You're the subject of tales, an example of a successful spycatcher, buster of enemies of the state, within and without—"

"A group effort!" She waived her hand to dismiss the undeserved praise. "I was merely acting on intelligence provided by the Company. The enemies of the state whom I am credited with exposing were some of the Company's deadliest enemies. It was quite ingenious. Why bloody our hands if we could make our enemy carry out the dirty job? The Company provided and planted the evidence against those who were particularly nasty, and out I went to bust them. Then the likes of Kachem arrested them and disposed of—"

They sat quietly for a time. Then Dorn asked, "Have you ever thought of remarrying?"

She looked into his eyes.

"Thought? Certainly. I *thought* about it."

"Why didn't you?"

"Same reason you are not married."

"What makes you think I'm not married?"

"For one thing I did a background check on you, at least the legend created for the benefit of your employers. As far as your work for the cause… Could you ever devote yourself so wholly if you were a husband, a father? You are not an ordained priest, and I am not a sister, but for all intents and purposes, we are married to the Company. As such we practice celibacy— well—" she stumbled. "At least as far as organized marriage—"

"Many Fathers do not believe celibacy is the right answer," Dorn picked up. "'It's a factory for madmen', as some have put it."

"It does not seem effective when forced upon," she agreed. "Keep in mind, though, that celibacy is often chosen, even among the general laic society, to help one focus on one's goals."

"Perhaps, then, it should be a matter of personal choice."

"Perhaps," she said.

They fell silent for a time.

"Tell me something, Kamil," the woman opened. "You are as devoted to the Company as any Father. How come you did not pursue your priestly education? How come you did not take the vows, but joined the Invisible Company instead?"

"I suppose, you might say, I have something in common with Kachem."

"Oh?" her brows arched.

He winked mischievously and said, "We both get a kick from quick results."

45. Curtain Rises

Dorn's mobile vibrated. A glance at the screen tensed the muscles of his face. His eyes sent a silent message across the air to Father Giordano. He showed the screen to the woman, who nodded, and picked up her own mobile phone. She keyed in a number, and exchanged several words with the recipient in a coquettish tone of voice Dorn could not imagine her capable of several days ago. She hung up and looked at her companion. No words were necessary to convey the message that the bait was swallowed.

The first stage of the plan was set into motion.

Hollie stayed in place, while Dorn crossed the street and approached the restaurant patio where a colorful rancher laughed gregariously to a lewd joke told by the Gringo. Dorn was fascinated by an image of Kachem he never saw before. Intoxicated, the Major actually resembled a human being, relaxed, outgoing, and receptive to others around him. The two men seemed the best of friends, so much so that Dorn worried his superior officer might have had too much too drink for the play he was about to witness and participate in. Another burst of laughter, this time on the part of the officer, and to an anecdote told by the elder, reassured him that all was on the right path.

"Dorn! I swear you are avoiding me!" Kachem noticed his subordinate's presence only when he towered over the table.

"On the contrary. I was hoping to find you here—" Dorn replied in a tone of voice that spelled urgency.

"You're baiting me!" His eyes suddenly alert, Kachem appeared sober save for the slur in his voice. "You found the —" he checked himself, and looked across the table, to the suddenly inconvenient presence of his binging companion. He jolted to his feet, and in the process knocked over the bottle. He grasped Dorn's elbow and led him into a large potted plant near the hotel entrance, or so he thought, for in reality it was the younger man who led the way.

"Tell me. Now!"

Dorn said what was agreed upon, "Capt. Weader met with the courier."

"And? And? Go on, man!"

"She had a bad feeling, wanted me to tag along as her back up. The exchange happened on a remote stretch of highway, way up. The courier took the drive and disappeared."

"Did he say anything?"

"He was not in a chatty mood, besides everything happened very quickly."

Kachem gripped his arm, perhaps from anxiety, perhaps to balance on his uncertain legs.

"What did he look like?"

Dorn had not prepared for this question.

He replied after a moment's hesitation, "Plain, unremarkable. We had no time to take a closer look. In any case, the whole thing happened too quickly."

"Of course! The bastards learned their trade. But can you make him out?"

"Why? Don't we want the courier to deliver the Trojan Horse?"

"It doesn't hurt to know who's who!"

"I don't know. The sun was setting directly behind his back, blinding us, his body a silhouette."

Kachem cursed.

"The Devil's on their side! They ought to call themselves the Company of the Devil, not Jesus!"

He cursed some more before inquiring about the woman.

"She's keeping en eye on—"

"The mole!" Kachem caught on instantly, his hand squeezing Dorn's elbow. "You found the mole!"

Dorn made his first mistake. His eyes glazed over Kachem's shoulder to the hotel entrance. It was the unmistakable glance of avoidance, which every cop was trained to detect. Kachem would have, too, had he not been under the influence of alcohol and heightened anxiety. Perhaps he would have followed Dorn's gaze, which was just as well that he did not, for he would have scared off the man who appeared at the door.

With his back to the entrance, covering Dorn from the sight of the passerby, Kachem pulled closer, and hissed, "Give him to me!"

"You will get your mole, a swine who deserves what's coming!" Dorn replied in a voice that added fuel to fire.

"Now, Dorn! Now!" Kachem's grip tightened on Kamil's elbow.

The bells rang the hour, momentarily diverting Kachem's attention. It was all the time Dorn needed. He freed himself from the grip, and awaiting sufficient time for the newly arrived to pass them, he stepped forward. He watched as the man approached the curb, evidently eying someone across the street. Dorn's heart raced. This was it. The crucial moment in his plan had come. The main actor had arrived on the scene, playing his role according to the screenplay concocted ad hoc and not written in stone, leaving plenty of room for improvisation. Dorn's eyes glided over the man's bulky shoulders, across the street, to the woman who stood under a lamppost, the bait. Her flirtatious voice had drawn the predator out of his den. His appetite for the prey was equal to Kachem's appetite for the mole.

"Helborn!" Dorn called out.

46. The Ghost Effect

To say that Foras Helborn was shocked would grossly underestimate the effect of seeing a ghost. Helborn's awe at hearing the voice of the dead was absolute. He had rushed out of the hotel under the premise of a date with the dashing woman, only to face the ghost of the one he never expected to see again. The shock was the more striking for he knew the ghost was not a ghost at all. Ghosts did not talk. Frozen in place he could not bring himself to turn around to face the man whom he saw plunge to his death.

Dorn took several steps forward, leaving the stupefied Major behind. He spoke in a voice loud enough for both men to hear.

"You've disgraced the uniform your country clad you with!"

Helborn turned around, slowly, his face contorted, his body tense.

Everything hung by a thread. Helborn's reaction was the most crucial stage of the plan. How would he react?

Helborn did nothing.

Dorn was covered in cold sweat. He was faced with an unforeseen factor, one which could lay all his hopes in ruin. Do something! he cried in his mind, but Helborn did nothing, and Dorn was at a loss. He had to rouse the vile beast, yet his mind drew blank. He expected a certain amount of shock caused by his sudden appearance, but not startling to the point where the man froze, unable to move. If anything, Dorn expected a reaction, which would set the scene and put all actors in motion. Apparently his psychological assessment of the cocky man did not account for paralysis.

What Dorn did not realize, however, was something else had confused and startled the body-snatching treasure hunter. It was the appearance of the notorious mole buster, the successful spycatcher, the ruthless Maj. Kachem, whose face appeared from the shadows, and now stood side by side with Dorn. Helborn's mind worked frantically. Something was terribly wrong. A man who should be dead was in fact very alive. But there was something, and it was much worse. It was the man who stood next to the would-be-dead, and whose entire being emanated a burning desire to deliver sophisticated pain.

The doors opened behind Dorn, casting bright lights on the face of the man standing in front of him. The lights allowed him to see the eyes, set firmly on a point next to Dorn. He glanced quickly to his right, and realized what had thrown Helborn off balance. Kachem! Of course! This was it!

"It's over, Helborn!" he said coldly and deliberately. "*We* have figured you out—"

The use of the pronoun had an electrifying effect.

"No! You can't stop me!" the disgraced medic roared.

In one swift move he slipped his hand underneath the flap of his jacket, and drew out a pistol.

It tells something of a man who carries a weapon to a date, a thought shot through Dorn's mind.

"You cowardly scum!" he yelled.

Indeed, Helborn was the type of man who stabs in the back, but cowers in the face of full frontal confrontation. He half-raised the pistol but did not fire, his mind not completely gone, allowing him to register the presence of restaurant patrons and passersby, postponing the deadly intent.

"Your time's up!" Dorn shouted in an effort to rouse the man. He lifted his arm, and pointed his index finger at Helborn. He said coldly, "You will pay for your crimes!"

It was a combination of factors that made Helborn react the way he did. The clear accusations, the realization his secret was out, and the presence of the notorious Maj. Kachem, were all sharp pins that burst the balloon of Helborn's anxiety.

"No!" Helborn shouted, animal fury in his eyes.

Dorn was ready. As Helborn's arm began its final upward swing, Dorn delivered a kick to the outstretched wrist. The sound of the shot was muffled by a passing old truck, but the bullet whizzed between the two heads of the officers, and acted as a bucket of cold water on the drunken one.

It was not over, as Dorn had hoped it would not be. Helborn was not an average run of the mill man with a gun. He was a military medic who served in some of the most ugly theaters of war. He was an old bird who understood when his time was up, and he would not go down easily, clinging to freedom with all his might.

As his hand lost grip of the pistol, his arm in a continuing crescent motion, Helborn took advantage of the involuntary movement set forth by the kick. He allowed his body to make the full turn, and as he faced Dorn again, his left fist was ready.

A powerful blow, made the stronger by full motion impetus threw Dorn onto Maj. Kachem.

Scrambling on the ground, Dorn cried to his companion, his lips spewing blood,

"It's him! He is the man you are after!"

47. The Finale

Maj. Kachem watched the unfolding scene with sobering angst. He recognized the object of Dorn's attention, though time marked its passage on the plump man. Kachem remembered the medic of the notorious unit that became the stuff of rumors, to this day spoken about in whispers by the peasants whose family members lived to tell their mysterious abduction stories. *Los vampiros del órganos*, they were human and moral degenerates, universally despised by their military comrades, a stain on military honor. Kachem knew about them, he worked alongside them in Central America. He knew this one particularly well — he was the head of the unit that performed battlefield extractions. Those were times when Kachem's pride in the uniform had been cut and extracted along with the organs of the vampires' victims. He would not easily forget the medic with the highest intelligence clearance, armed with orders to sequester any prisoner of war whose value he deemed important for his — as they called it in those days — research on the effects on

231

the various weaponry used in the battlefield. Kachem knew the vampires snatched fallen militants' organs not only for their officially proscribed duties. He knew they worked on the side for private sponsors, too. And Kachem could do nothing about it. His anger with the medic, anger which went back nearly three decades, was no lesser today. Though their duties separated them, Kachem's path had crossed with the medic's on several occasions since. He knew the research continued, albeit under more humane conditions. He knew the medic no longer served with the special forces, not ostensibly, but rather switched to private enterprise, which was contracted by the military. How closely private contractors were intertwined with the military, Kachem was able to discern on several occasions when he ran into the medic inside the Building. He was always surrounded by expensive suits and highly decorated brass. His reach was high. Very high. This man Helborn seemed to have unrestricted access.

Whatever alcohol circulated in Maj. Kachem's veins, it evaporated at the realization of the identity of the man standing in front of him. With his access to the Building, this could indeed have been the mole. Dorn's accusation, shouted out loud, had caused a reaction, which left no doubt, and the discharged weapon reaffirmed Kachem's growing conviction.

"His name is Foras Helborn!" Dorn cried as he stumbled to his feet. "He has been using his unrestricted access to go in and out of the Building at will. He is the mole!"

"But now he's getting away!" Kachem gnawed his teeth, as he propped himself up. He watched as Helborn jumped into a car that was parked in front of the hotel and took off at high speed, maneuvering dangerously between moving vehicles.

"He won't!" Dorn said assertively.

Kachem did not notice his officer's peculiar conviction. It did not occur strange to him that a car should arrive at this moment, with a screech of tires, a rickety old sedan driven by Capt. Weader. He took the passenger seat without much ado and, with the window down, he kept his pistol ready.

"Don't you want him alive?" Dorn shouted over his shoulder as he took the wheel, and the woman moved to the back seat.

"Just get me close enough to aim for the tires!"

The Centro Historico was a maze of one way streets with no surprises awaiting the pursuers, making Helborn's escape route predictable. The trick was to catch up to him before the Avenida Panamericana, a busy roadway linking the Americas, in time to alert Father Giordano's guards who were ready at their posts. Hollie's thumb on the SEND button of her mobile phone, her eyes were glued to the runaway car. She waited until they reached an agreed location, and pushed the button just as Helborn reached a point on the thoroughfare, which would allow him to exit. She watched the effect of the sent text message — a pick-up jumpstarted from the side of the road, and cut off the speeding vehicle, forcing it to change lanes, and consequently sending it in the direction chosen by the pursuers. The same maneuver was repeated once again, at a crucial location, where the second of the guards ensured Helborn would chose the correct direction. Consequently the two vehicles found themselves climbing the serpent of the now familiar volcano.

The curving and narrow road, now completely deserted, for no daredevils would venture to try it after dark, it was, in Dorn's mind, ideal for the execution of the plan.

To Kachem's relief Dorn closed the distance between the cars. The Major waited for this moment too long. Undoubtedly feeling the change in altitude, yet unaware of the dangerous scenery on this pitch black night, he stuck his arm out the window, and aimed.

"Wait!" Dorn's voice prevented the discharge of the firearm.

"He's getting away!" Kachem would not have it.

"Aim for the tires!"

"Goddamnit, Dorn! Whatcha think I was doing!?"

Dorn smiled. When all was said and done his concern would be noted.

Helborn reached the narrowest curve, the same which nearly claimed Dorn's life. Now both vehicles seemed to travel in opposite direction, with only a narrow, if dark, void between them.

Kachem squeezed the trigger. Then again. And again.

Helborn's vehicle spun out of control.

"What the hell!" Kachem cried.

In the dark, with only the headlights visible, the car appeared to take flight. The sensation was the more striking for the downward arch the vehicle followed. Maj. Kachem could not believe his eyes. He followed the flight wide eyed, his shock so absolute he did not cover them when the vehicle burst into a huge ball of fire.

Dorn hit the breaks.

Kachem jumped out first. Only now did it occur to him what the night hid under its dark veil. In his agitated state of mind he did not associate the ascent with risk of losing the fugitive. He stood helpless on what appeared a bottomless pit, watching the vehicle burn down below. What thoughts ran through the officer's mind one could surmise from the complete silence, so unbecoming of the cursing man, eager to express his displeasure as part of a tactic to unsettle his victims. He awaited resignedly for the arrival of the firefighters and the police. He observed as the security service took over the operation of extracting the remains of the charred vehicle and its occupants, for there were two — one at the wheel, and another in the trunk. The latter was soon identified as the fearless and heroic Chief del Toro, who, according to official statements later released, fell victim to terrorist militants of the mountains.

Maj. Kachem remained stoic throughout the investigation, even when forensic experts found a small electronic device, or rather only what was left of it, the metal parts of a digital memory disk. If Kachem had any doubts about the identity of the mole they were now laid to rest. His long-held hate for the vile activities of the disgraced medic fed Kachem's desire to find the mole. The Major would have loved nothing more than to lay his hands on Helborn, whose body-snatching had cost the intelligence officer valuable prisoners. He regretted the death, which he considered a too easy a way out, one which did not teach other traitors to expect fate much worse once Maj. Kachem set his sights on them.

Dorn suffered no qualms about Helborn's demise. Given the medic's long career in the business of causing pain, death was indeed an easy and just way to end the wretched string of activities. All the same Dorn did not rejoice. The sum of too many terrifying memories of his own experiences, as well as those of his friends, had stripped him of the basic emotion that was satisfaction of seeing his enemy fall. He did not find closure in the death of the death squad commander, either. Having spent much of his young life in the battle for change he had learned that punishing the executors did not end evil policies. He knew he could not achieve the change he vied for without attacking the root of the evil. Brother Anselm was right in their frequent discussions, when denouncing violence as the answer. Dorn agreed with his mentor, and everything he witnessed in his service for a better world had confirmed it. But he was young when he joined the service. He did not posses the philosophical patience of his elders. He wanted justice here and now. As he stood now, at the precipice, his hand embracing the hand of the woman, he was stricken with as much gratification as a feeling of helplessness. The deaths of Helborn and del Toro fed his hunger for the time being, but he knew he would it would never fully satisfy him. Not for as long as there existed a system that allowed such men to operate. He understood his chosen path was a vicious circle. A circle whose center of gravity kept him as though on a leash, from which he could not break free. He would not to attempt it. It was no longer within his power. He was a satellite circling around a large and growing body of good. Someday the body would engulf the smaller, but highly charged body of evil. Meanwhile he would remain at its orbit, helping to usher in the growing tides of change.

AMEN

From the Author

Agents of Change is a novel of suspense, a pinhole into a monumental and immensely complicated struggle for a better world. Because of the constraints of the genre, and in the interest of reading flow, many aspects of the work of the agents of change were either omitted, or were only alluded to, on the pages of this book.

Curious readers are encouraged to seek further material concerning progressive Catholic priests — Agents of Change — in relation to Liberation Theology. Involved in the struggle for a better world were, among others, Franciscans and the Society of Jesus, or the Company of Jesus, better known as Jesuits, whose efforts were strengthened by the decisions of the Second Vatican Council (Vatican II), with its "preferential option for the poor", which terrified the Vatican Hierarchy and the United States, alike. Indeed, Liberation Theology was deemed by the U.S. military intelligence to pose the biggest threat to American interests: Barely two months after his election, President Ronald

Reagan met with the National Security Council to discuss one thing: How to destroy Liberation Theology. They did not succeed, but they were successful in dividing the Church.

The struggle continues today, and some of the demands of the agents of change include, but are not limited to…

Demands for:

The abolition of the priestly character of the Jesuit Order; Abolition of the Church Hierarchy; Diminished role of the Pope; The end of Celibacy…

Questioning of:

Papal infallibility; The Existence of Heaven and Hell; The Immaculate Conception…

Acceptance of:

Contraception; Abortion; Homosexuality; Premarital sex; Masturbation…

Fight against:

Consumerism; Globalization; Market economy…

Support For:

Priesthood for Women; Organizing workers' unions; Low cost housing; Microloans; Microcredit; Political demonstrations; Political advocacy; Nationalization of industries; Preferential Option for the Poor; Creation of Base Communities; Worker Priests…

The picture would not be complete without further reading on:

Father General Pedro Arrupe; Red Jesuits; Red Bishops; Red Cardinals; El Salvador; UCA; Death Squads; SOA; School of Americas; Archbishop Oscar Romero; Jesuit Vows: Three Vows / Four Vows; Decree Four of the 32nd General Congregation

About the Author

As a former top-secret government courier, Jack King was privy to all the ins and outs of covert maneuvering on a global scale. He has turned his work experience into a series of novels that resonate with authenticity. The corridors of power, with their backstabbing, greed, and corruption, are the focus points of Jack's books:

Agents of Change: With its antiquated political and banking systems, rogue military-industrial complexes and flawed educational systems, the world of today is a relic of the imperfect past, and Agents of Change are ready to right what is wrong.

WikiJustice: There exists a place where no one stands above the law, where individuals and corporations are held liable in ways, which fit their crimes... WikiJustice.

The Black Vault: Secret funds, obtained by illicit means, used for the purpose of conducting black operations.

In the 1930s a group of wealthy industrialists plotted to overthrow President Franklin D. Roosevelt and replace him with a puppet dictator. The coup failed because of moral reservations of a single man.

Can one man stop a conspiracy to overthrow the current-day President?

The Fifth Internationale: Now that the Iron Curtain had come crushing down, and Soviet satellite countries switched allegiance to the United States, their communist spies are no longer needed. Hundreds of thousands are discharged, but not retired - they form The Fifth Internationale, building a global conspiracy that will allow them to manipulate world governments to their own end.

Please point your browser to **SpyWriter.com** to connect with the author.

www.ingramcontent.com/pod-product-compliance
Lightning Source LLC
Chambersburg PA
CBHW070918180626
46817CB00003B/1122